'Why don't we go for a swim in the moonlight, Leo?'

There was silence, and Amelie felt colour rise in her cheeks. He'd asked her round for a meal—not to go down to the beach.

He had come to stand beside her, and into the silence that had followed her suggestion said, 'Yes—why not? I've done it before, and no doubt will do it again. It's a fantastic feeling. If you pop across and change into your swimming gear I'll do the same, and will meet you out at the front in ten minutes, OK?'

The tide was coming in less vigorously than it sometimes did, and as they swam in its unaccustomed gentleness, with moonlight throwing shadows on the rocks and the sand that the sea hadn't yet reached, there was a tranquillity that they could both feel.

Amelie was so entranced by the magic of the evening that she fantasised about her role as temporary doctor leading to a permanent position. It would be one way of staying in Bluebell Cove—something she was increasingly keen to do…

Dear Reader

Here we have Amelie and Leo's story—the last of my quartet of books set in Bluebell Cove, a beautiful coastal village in 'glorious' Devon.

If you have read WEDDING BELLS FOR THE VILLAGE NURSE, the first of my four books about this village by the sea, you will have already met Jenna and Lucas. In CHRISTMAS IN BLUEBELL COVE we had Francine and Ethan's story, followed by THE VILLAGE NURSE'S HAPPY-EVER-AFTER, which told of Phoebe and Harry's search for happiness. Now, between the pages of SUMMER SEASIDE WEDDING, we are once again sharing the lives and loves of the folk who live in Bluebell Cove.

Until we meet again, I do wish you happy reading.

With best wishes

Abigail Gordon

SUMMER SEASIDE WEDDING

BY
ABIGAIL GORDON

First published in Great Britain 2011
by Mills & Boon,
an imprint of Harlequin (UK) Limited,
Large Print edition 2011
Eton House, 18-24 Paradise Road,
Richmond, Surrey TW9 1SR

© Abigail Gordon 2011

ISBN: 978 0 263 21758 2

Harlequin (UK) policy is to use papers that are
natural, renewable and recyclable products and made
from wood grown in sustainable forests. The logging
and manufacturing process conform to the legal
environmental regulations of the country of origin.

Printed and bound in Great Britain
by CPI Antony Rowe, Chippenham, Wiltshire

Abigail Gordon loves to write about the fascinating combination of medicine and romance from her home in a Cheshire village. She is active in local affairs, and is even called upon to write the script for the annual village pantomime! Her eldest son is a hospital manager, and helps with all her medical research. As part of a close-knit family, she treasures having two of her sons living close by, and the third one not too far away. This also gives her the added pleasure of being able to watch her delightful grandchildren growing up.

Recent titles by the same author:

CHAPTER ONE

IT WAS June and the hot summer sun above made the confines of the car feel restricting as Leo Fenchurch drove along the road at the top of the cliffs in Bluebell Cove, a coastal village in the Devonshire countryside.

It had been a long morning. The first surgery of the day had been followed by home visits to the patients of the Tides Practice, where he was employed as one of the two doctors there, and now every time he glanced down at the sea, blue and dazzling as it danced onto the sandy beach, his collar felt tighter, his smart suit more a burden than an asset, and the yearning to pull into a deserted lay-by and change into the swimming trunks he always carried in the car was strong.

But needless to say he couldn't give in to the temptation. After a hasty lunch there would be the second surgery of the day to cope with and by the time that was over it would be half past six, so any sun-worshipping and bathing would have to wait until a summer evening unfolded.

The practice was on the road he was driving along, past the headland overlooking the sea, and situated in the centre of the village. As he drove onto the forecourt the red car belonging to Harry Balfour, the senior partner, pulled up alongside.

As the two men walked towards the main entrance to the surgery Harry said, 'There is something I need to discuss with you, Leo, before we grab a bite of lunch, so let's go to my room, shall we?'

'Yes, sure.' The fair-haired six-footer, who was top of the list of Bluebell Cove's most eligible men, had no problems with that.

The two of them worked well together, especially since Harry had recently married Phoebe and now seemed in a permanent state of bliss. He was a changed man from the brusque widower who'd returned from Australia to take over the practice. And the change in him was all due to meeting the love of his life after a marriage that had not been the most satisfying of relationships.

Phoebe Morgan had been the district nurse attached to the practice but was now no longer employed there because she was expecting their first baby, a brother or sister for Marcus, her son from her own disastrous previous marriage and a child that Harry loved as if he was his own.

A carefree playboy himself when he wasn't at the surgery, Leo had thought a few times when observing his partner's contentment that maybe he was missing out by never committing himself to any of the opposite sex who were ever ready to be in his company given the chance.

But the woman had yet to appear who could make the most attractive man in Bluebell Cove want to settle down. Once long ago he'd thought he'd found her, but a force stronger than either of them had decreed that it was not to be.

'I had a phone call from Ethan while I was out on my rounds,' Harry explained once they were seated in his office.

Leo observed him questioningly. It had only been a few weeks since Ethan Lomax, who had been in charge of the practice before Harry had come and now lived in France, had brought his family over for the wedding of the man sitting opposite, so what was it now?

He was soon to find out. 'As you know, Ethan is working in a French hospital,' Harry explained, 'and has been approached by a junior doctor who is keen to get some experience of general practice, British style. Willing to assist if possible, he rang to ask if we could fit this person into the practice here for a few months. I told him I couldn't just say yes on the spur of the moment without discussing it with you, and would get back to him. So, what do you think?'

'An extra pair of hands would come in useful,' Leo said slowly, 'but how experienced is this guy?'

Harry was smiling. 'What makes you think it's a man?'

'So it's a woman?'

'Yes. Her name is Amelie Benoir. She's twenty-six years old and was top of her course at medical school, so I feel that an extra doctor in the practice for a while and one of such promise is too good an opportunity to miss, but first I want *your* opinion, Leo.'

'I feel the same as you,' Leo told him, 'and if this Benoir woman is what Ethan says with regard to ability *and* is as chic as his French wife, Francine, it will be a double bonus.'

'You never change, do you?' Harry commented with wry amusement, but Leo didn't rise to the bait. His mind was on the practicalities of the idea.

'So where would this French doctor stay?' he questioned, and then reverting back to form, went on, 'How about the apartment next to mine above the surgery? It worked for you and Phoebe when the two of you lived up there, didn't it?'

'I thought you weren't the marrying kind,' was Harry's reply to that.

'Who said anything about marrying? But I have to admit I envy you sometimes.'

'That is because I've found the right one,' he was told, 'and, having said that, going home to Phoebe and Marcus is the highlight of my day, so if this Amelie Benoir does come to join us here, I'd be obliged if you would go to the airport to meet her if she arrives in the evening. If it's during the day I'll do the honours, though evening would be better all round, I feel.

'Besides, with only the two of us as GPs, it's tough when one of us is missing, so I'll mention that to Ethan when I return his call and suggest she flies in after the surgeries, unless she's already found herself a niche over here by the time he speaks to her again. If she hasn't, and does come to join us for a while, I'm afraid she won't be living in the apartment across from yours. Ethan has offered to let her rent his house in the village at a nominal sum for however long she stays.'

The following morning Harry announced that he and his predecessor had spoken the night before and arrangements were already in hand for the temporary addition to the practice to join them the following week.

She was to arrive next Friday evening, which would allow her time to get used to her new surroundings before presenting herself at the surgery on Monday morning.

Leo would meet her at the airport and give her the keys to Ethan's house, and Harry and Phoebe would make sure that a bed was made up and there was food in the fridge.

Having taken note of the arrangements, Leo put the new arrival out of his mind until such time as it had been arranged he should be at the airport to meet her. He carried on with his leisure pursuits as normal, which included swim-ming at every opportunity, tennis, and taking part in the village's social life in the form of dining out and attending local entertainment.

When Lucy, the elderly practice nurse who had worked at the surgery for as long as anyone could remember, asked him one morning if the trainee doctor was married or single, coming alone or accompanied, Leo had to tell her that he didn't know, hadn't thought to ask. Neither, it seemed, had Harry.

He appeared at that moment and when con-sulted merely said, 'Ethan's house is big enough to accommodate eight to ten people comfortably, so there won't be a problem regarding anyone she brings with her.'

'Especially if she's got lots of attractive sis-ters,' Leo joked, and Lucy smiled. She liked Leo Fenchurch, liked his easy manner, which some people misread. In reality he was a caring and experienced doctor who often concealed his feelings behind a casual bonhomie, which could be the reason why so many of the local female population sought his company.

Leo set off for the airport the moment the surgeries of the day were over on the Friday of the following week. It was a lengthy drive and he had no wish for the new arrival to be without someone to greet her when the aircraft touched down, which meant that he was still wearing the suit he wore for the practice, having had no time to change, and was hungry into the bargain, again because of the time factor.

Amelie Benoir's name was printed in large capitals on a piece of cardboard beside him on the passenger seat of the car and he was hoping that she would be one of the first off the plane so that he could take her for something to eat to appease his hunger.

The traffic wasn't good, but Friday nights never were, he thought as he watched the minutes ticking by. He strode into the arrivals lounge holding his piece of cardboard aloft with only seconds to spare as the first passengers from the French flight began to filter through.

His eyes widened. It looked as if his wishes were going to be granted. This had to be her, he thought as a tall, elegant woman with a sweep of shining blonde hair appeared amongst the first of the arrivals.

He reached out over the barrier as she drew level and held the card out for her to see, but there was no reaction, just a rather surprised smile and then she was gone, moving in the direction of the taxi rank. So much for that, he thought wryly. He'd been too quick off the mark there.

Passengers kept coming and no one stepped out of line and claimed to be Amelie Benoir. Eventually he was the only one there with his piece of card. As the last two, a rather nondescript couple, appeared, he was on the point of turning away when the woman called, 'Wait, please. I am she. I am Amelie Benoir.' As he observed her in dismayed surprise, the man that he'd thought she was with proceeded to the nearest exit.

He almost groaned out loud at the idea of mistaking the other woman for this untidy creature, but pulling himself together he said smoothly, 'Welcome to Devon, Dr Benoir. I am Leo Fenchurch, one of the doctors in the practice. If you will walk to the end of the barrier, I will take charge of your luggage, and then perhaps you would like some refreshment before we embark on what is quite a long drive to Bluebell Cove.'

It had been a shift like most of the shifts for junior doctors at the busy hospital where Amelie had first met the friendly Ethan Lomax. Who had set her imagination on fire when he'd spoken of the beautiful village on the coast of Devon where he'd lived before moving to France.

She had been allotted to Women's Surgical and had been nearing the end of what should have been a twelve-hour shift, but as sometimes happened it had been twice as long for various reasons, and for the last couple of hours Amelie had cast frequent glances at the clock because she hadn't wanted to miss her flight to the UK. If its relentless hands hadn't messed up her arrangements, there had always been the chance that exhaustion would.

But release had come at last and hurrying to her flat, which fortunately had been in the staff accommodation part of the hospital complex, she'd thrown off her hospital garb, showered, and replaced the clothes she'd taken off with the only jacket and trousers she possessed for travelling in.

Picking up her case, which fortunately she'd packed previously, she'd hailed a taxi from the rank outside the hospital gates and the last thing she remembered after settling into her seat on the plane had been wishing that it wasn't going to be such a short flight as the exhaustion that she'd had to fight to get there on time had taken over and even before take-off she'd been asleep.

It was why she was one of the last off the aircraft, drowsy and disorientated. She saw the card in the hand of a man who looked like the angel Gabriel in a suit and wished that she'd managed to find time to brush her hair properly instead of just rubbing it dry with the towel after she'd showered.

She was discovering that his likeness to an angel wasn't just in the golden fairness of him. He was offering her food and as it had been hours since she'd eaten, she would have kissed his feet if he'd asked her to. Yet there was nothing angelic about the hand that he'd extended to shake her ringless one. The contact was brief, but she felt a firmness and sense of purpose in its clasp.

'Yes, please,' she said in reply to his offer of food. 'I'm famished. I came straight off my shift with only a short time to spare before my flight was due to leave, and have slept all the way.'

He nodded. At that moment she looked like what she was, an overworked, underpaid junior doctor with the white mask of exhaustion that most of them wore.

The rest of her was made up of hair that was black as raven's wings in a short cut that would have looked stylish if she'd taken the trouble to run a comb through it, and there was a snub nose in the centre of a face with a wide mouth that looked as if it might smile a lot under other circumstances.

She was of average height, average weight, everything about her was average, except for her eyes. They made up for it, blue as the bluebells that the village got its name from, and as their glances met, his keen and perceptive and hers still verging on sleep, he thought that maybe she wouldn't be such a disappointment after all. If nothing else, she would be an extra pair of hands.

He took her to eat in a restaurant on the airport concourse and as she enjoyed the food he reflected it was only the smell and sight of it that was keeping her awake.

A visit to the powder room followed the meal and Amelie sighed at the vision she presented in the mirror there. A quick flick of a comb through her hair improved it slightly, but the overall effect was far from how she would have wanted to appear on arriving in the UK for the first time to be met by a man who on closer inspection was more like a Greek god than an angel, but so what? She was off men, had been ever since she'd given Antoine his ring back.

The hurt and humiliation of what he'd done to her had made her feel unlovely and unloved when it had happened, but she felt she was over that now, had risen above those sort of feelings, and been grateful in a crazy sort of way for the long hours and other demands made of a junior doctor, which had left her with little time to brood. Yet it would be an eternity before she put her trust in or gave her heart to another of his sex.

Leo was waiting for her by the reception desk with her cases beside him when she reappeared, and didn't miss the fact that the black bob of her hair now hung smooth and shining around her face.

That's better, he thought, and almost laughed at the workings of his mind.

Amelie Benoir hadn't crossed the Channel to enter a beauty competition. She'd come to gain some experience in general practice and hope-fully give assistance to Harry and himself at the same time.

'Thanks for the food,' she said gratefully. 'I feel much better now.'

'Good. I was a junior doctor myself once and remember the trials and tribulations just as much as the rewards. So if you want to nod off again feel free because it will be some time before we arrive in Bluebell Cove.'

'What is the house like where I shall be living?' she asked after they'd travelled the first few miles in silence, each not sure if the other wanted to talk.

'It was built for Ethan and his family a couple

of years ago and is very spacious and attractive. It is opposite the surgery so you won't have to travel to get there. With regard to visiting our patients, Dr. Balfour is sorting out a hire car for you, though you will be with one of us until you know the district and have got the hang of the surgery routine.'

'And where do you live?' was her next question.

'Nowhere as sumptuous as where you will be living in Ethan's modern detached, or Harry Balfour's manor house,' he said laughingly. 'I live in an apartment above the surgery that supplies my needs.'

'So you do not have family?'

'My mother is alive. She lives in Spain with my sister and her husband. I'm not married myself, neither do I have any children. Families are the ties that bind, I feel. What about you? Have you left family behind in France?'

She shook her head and he thought there was something sad about the gesture. 'No. I have not left anyone behind. Both my parents are in the diplomatic service and spend most of their time abroad. I rarely see them.'

He nodded, 'I only asked because Ethan's house is big. If you'd wanted to bring anyone with you, he wouldn't have minded.'

'I might have done at one time,' she replied, 'but not now.' Silence fell between them once more.

It was gone midnight when Leo pulled up across the way from the surgery in front of the big detached house that was to be her home for the next six months.

Amelie had been half-asleep on the last leg of the journey but had woken up when he'd turned onto the coast road and been tuned in when he'd explained that the sea and the beach were below and that a house standing on a headland overlooking them called Four Winds because of its exposed position was occupied by a frail elderly woman who had once been in charge of the medical practice that they were heading for.

'I have lived in many places,' she told him, 'and the ones I have liked best were always beside the ocean. So this is a great adventure for me.'

'That's good, then,' he commented as he took her cases out of the boot and carried them to the front door of the house. While he was unlocking it he said, 'Ethan and his family were here just a few weeks ago for Harry and Phoebe's wedding, so all should be in order.' And with her close behind, he led the way inside.

Amelie looked around her, wide eyed at the spacious rooms and attractive, modern furniture, and Leo thought that this place made the apartment above the surgery look like a henhouse, yet did it matter? It was enough for his needs at the present time.

'If you would like to take a look upstairs, you should find that Phoebe has made up one of the beds for you, and there will be fresh food in the cupboards and the refrigerator,' he explained. 'If you need anything over the weekend, you know where to find me, above the surgery.'

'You will see a separate staircase leading to the apartment and there is a buzzer by the door. Now I shall leave you to settle in.' With a glance at her tired face, he added, 'Sleep well. Harry and Phoebe will be calling in to introduce themselves some time over the weekend and, as I've said, I won't be far away, so I'll say goodnight until eight-thirty on Monday morning.'

'Thank you for bringing me here, Dr Fenchurch,' she said, and he sensed the melancholy in her tone again.

Yet she was smiling as she went to the door to see him off and nodded obediently when he said, 'Be sure to lock and bolt the doors after I've gone.'

It was only when she was alone in the strange house that she'd escaped to that she allowed herself to think that with midnight already past, today should have been her wedding day.

Had Antoine even remembered, she wondered,

or was he so engrossed in his new love that he'd shut the past out of his mind? Whatever the answer to that was, *she* was here in this beautiful English village and was going to make the most of the time by helping the sick and enjoying the change of surroundings, and along with that was hoping to find some kind of permanent healing for her own hurts.

She awoke the next morning to the sound of shrill cries in the distance and when she went to the window Amelie saw gulls circling around the headland.

There was a clear blue sky and already the sun was out, warm and tempting overhead, even though it was only six o'clock. So tempting that instead of going back to bed and allowing herself the treat of a lie-in, the urge to explore her new surroundings was strong.

Within a very short time she'd breakfasted on some of the wholesome-looking food that had been left for her, had had a shower, and was striding along towards the beach in shorts and a cotton top to conceal a bikini, with a towel over her arm.

It wasn't just curiosity that was taking her there. It was a day that Amelie intended to fill with everything except thoughts of what might have been. Exploring Bluebell Cove was top of the list, and wallowing in hurtful memories at the bottom.

When she passed the house called Four Winds an elderly man was pottering around the garden and he gave a friendly wave when she appeared. The strip of golden sand below was deserted and as the sea pounded against the rocks and the gulls continued to screech above, she was out of the shorts and top and walking barefoot towards the water's edge in a matter of seconds, as if the wide expanse of ocean was a huge blue magnet pulling her towards it.

Leo had seen her go by from his vantage point above the surgery and had watched her walking towards the beach in amazement. Where was the exhausted young doctor of the previous night? he thought, never having dreamt that she would be up and about so early.

Getting her to Bluebell Cove and dropping her at Ethan's house had been enough to be going on with after a busy day in the surgery with journeys to and from the airport added on, so issuing warnings about dangerous currents and rip tides hadn't been in his mind at gone midnight the night before.

For one thing, he hadn't been expecting her to surface before midday and there she was, moving towards the delights of the cove with a spring in her step, which was more than he could say for himself.

He would have mentioned the tides if he'd had time to think the night before, but having not done so he couldn't let her go down there with no such thoughts in her mind. Within seconds he was following her, dressed in a similar manner in shorts and a T-shirt with swimwear underneath, and feeling less than chirpy at not having fulfilled his function as welcome party to Amelie Benoir.

She was in the water when he got there, swimming effortlessly quite a way out, and he groaned. He could murder a coffee and some toast, followed by a leisurely read of the morning paper, but first he was going to have to swim out to her, explain the dangers, and suggest that she swim nearer to the shore as Ronnie, the lifeguard, didn't appear on the beach until eight o'clock. The treacherous tides only surfaced rarely but strangers and locals alike needed to be aware of them.

When he bobbed up beside her in the water he gestured for her to swim back to the beach with him, and when they were on the sand she exclaimed, 'Dr Fenchurch! Do you also like to swim at this time of day?'

'Not unless I have to,' he told her dryly. 'I saw

you walking past my place and came to warn you that there are dangerous tides on rare occasions that you need to be aware of. I should have mentioned it last night, but wasn't expecting you to be out and about so early after your exhaustion of yesterday.'

'Yes, I know,' she said apologetically, 'but my room was full of sunlight and I could hear the gulls. I just had to explore down here.'

She wasn't going to tell him that today she didn't want time to think, that she needed to be occupied every moment so that her thoughts wouldn't be of a wedding dress taken back to the shop, a bridal cake that had to be cancelled, and on a larger scale a honeymoon that hadn't materialised.

'So can I expect you to be watchful?' he asked, about to depart.

'Yes, of course. I will take note of everything that you say.'

'Good, and now I'm going back for some

breakfast. Enjoy your weekend, Amelie.' And off he went with the thought going round in his mind that there was a solitariness about her that was worrying.

As he settled down to a belated breakfast and the morning paper, Leo was hoping the new addition to the practice would find her own niche socially and workwise, and that his part in the proceedings would now be completed.

He could understand her eagerness to go down to the beach and having seen her swim understood why. She moved like a dream in the water, and now he supposed she would be exploring the rest of Bluebell Cove if she hadn't gone back to bed. He hoped that Harry and Phoebe would take up where he'd left off and make her feel welcome.

For his own day he'd arranged to spend time on the tennis courts later in the morning with Naomi, an aspiring fashion model. On Saturday afternoons he always drove into town, and tonight was joining Georgina, the attractive owner of the local boutique, and her friends for a meal. So *his* day was planned.

Amelie hadn't gone back to bed. She'd considered it, but knew that alone in the stillness of the bedroom the thoughts she was trying to keep in check would come sweeping over her and she would be lost.

Instead, she was going to explore the shops in the main street of the village, then walk as far as she could see on the road that ran along the top of the cliffs. And somewhere in the midst of her exploring she would eat.

The 'Angel Gabriel' hadn't seemed too cheerful when he'd found her already in the sea at just gone six o'clock in the morning, but she was afraid he would have to get used to that because she loved to swim; and if life at the village practice was as demanding as the job she'd just left, it might be her only chance at that early hour.

So far she hadn't met the senior partner but

there was plenty of time for that. She'd met Leo, that was enough to be going on with, and for the rest of the weekend she wasn't going to butt into his life again.

The shops were to her liking. They reminded her of those in the French village where she'd lived as a child. Amongst them was a grocer's selling butter straight from the tub, a fishmonger's with the morning's fresh catch on display, and a combined village store and post office where people were good-humouredly passing the time of day without seeming to be in any hurry.

There was the feeling of life lived at a slower pace, she thought as she set off in the direction of the cliffs and the road that ran along the top of them. As she breathed in the fresh sea air and felt the sun on her face Amelie knew she'd done the right thing in accepting Ethan's suggestion that she come to Bluebell Cove *and she was here today of all days.*

She could see the sea in the distance as she

walked along. The tide had gone out and there were more people down on the sand now than there had been earlier. She was in love with the place already, she thought wonderingly. What must it be like to live here all the time?

When she looked over her shoulder she was surprised to see how far she'd walked. The village was almost out of sight and having no wish to make her arrival in Bluebell Cove brought to the notice of others by getting lost, she began to retrace her steps.

Eventually she came to tennis courts that had been empty when she'd passed earlier but were now occupied by an attractive blonde with long legs. Partnering her, resplendent in tennis shorts and a short-sleeved white shirt, was the man she'd been hoping to avoid for the rest of the weekend.

Fortunately he was serving with his back to her and with a few fast steps she was past before he'd had the chance to see her.

She was smiling as she neared the edge of the

village. It made sense that a man like him would want someone as attractive as himself to have around him, she was thinking when suddenly the church bells began to ring out and as she drew nearer the reason was revealed.

A June bride, resplendent in a beautiful white dress and train, was being helped out of a wedding car that had stopped at the lychgate of the church, and Amelie felt as if a cloud had covered the sun.

So much for upbeat thinking and keeping occupied on this particular day. Who was she kidding? The hurt hadn't gone away. She'd learned to live with it, but it was still there.

Turning away blindly, she hurried past the shops until she came to a café and seated herself at a table farthest from the window.

CHAPTER TWO

THE tennis had been good, his companion pleasant to be with, and as the two of them walked along the main street of the village, seeking refreshment after the exercise, Leo was aware that the bells were ringing at the church and a wedding was taking place.

Not an unusual event on a Saturday in June, by any means, but it was attracting a lot of attention, as weddings always did, and when his tennis partner wanted to linger outside the church they separated, him to the café farther along the street and her to join those who were waiting for the bride and her groom to appear.

The place was almost empty when he got there, even cream teas were being overshadowed by what was happening at the church, but there was one customer sitting at a table at the back, staring into space, and he forced a smile.

Hot and sticky, he just wanted to relax but she was here again, the young French doctor looking so forlorn he just had to go across and say hello.

'So how's it going?' he asked easily, towering above her with racket in hand.

'Fine,' she said with a pale smile.

'You must be the only one not watching what is going on at the church. I thought that most women love a wedding.'

He was making conversation and knew it, out of his depth because she looked so glum, and he was dumbstruck when she said tonelessly, 'Not those who have been betrayed. Today should have been my wedding day too. I should have been a bride, but as you can see it has not happened.'

'Oh!' he exclaimed, and lowered himself onto the chair beside her. 'I am so sorry. I would never have brought up the subject of marriage if I'd known. It is not surprising that you aren't amongst the observers and well-wishers. Do you want to talk about it?'

She shook her head. 'No, I don't, Dr Fenchurch. I was managing to get through the day reasonably well until I saw the wedding and came in here to get away from it.' The pale smile was back. 'But I'm all right now.' Steering the conversation into less upsetting channels, she said, 'What has happened to your tennis partner?'

'Naomi? She's outside the church with everyone else, but we were about to separate in any case. We only meet once weekly for tennis. So why don't you let me take you back to the house before the bridal couple appear?'

'But you came in here for some refreshment,' she protested.

'I'll have a bite when I've seen you safely away from all of this,' he replied. 'If we take the long way round we'll miss the church. But, Amelie, I have to warn you there will be other weddings. June is the most popular month in the year so...'

'I'm not going to have a panic attack every time I see one,' she told him.

'It was because it was today of all days that it upset me so much, and I'm butting into your weekend again, aren't I? I am so sorry.'

'Don't be. You are alone in a strange place and I am happy to help in any way I can,' he assured her, and was surprised how much he meant it. 'So let's go, shall we?' And with a smile for the girl behind the counter as Amelie paid for what she'd had, he shepherded her outside and they set off in the opposite direction from the wedding.

Harry had rung him after breakfast, wanting to know if the previous night's arrangements had gone smoothly, and he'd been able to tell him that they had.

'So what's she like?' he'd wanted to know, and Leo had described her briefly.

'Something in your tone tells me that Amelie is not another chic Francine Lomax,' the senior partner had said laughingly.

Leo hadn't taken him up on that comment. Instead, he'd told him, 'She was down in the cove swimming at some godless hour this morning after seeming to be completely exhausted last night.'

'How do you know that?'

'I saw her go past with a towel over her arm and realised I hadn't told her about the rip tides, so went after her to be on the safe side.'

'And where is she now?'

'I don't know, but if her rapture on seeing Bluebell Cove is anything to go by, she'll be out seeing the sights.'

'We'll be calling round soon,' Harry had informed him, 'and if she isn't there we can stop by again later.'

It would seem that she hadn't been there because she was here with him, Leo was thinking when the surgery and the house opposite came into view. When she opened the door there was a note behind it.

He was observing her hesitantly as she bent to

pick it up, undecided whether he should go and leave her to her private thoughts or offer to stay and keep her company for a while until he was sure she was all right to be left on her own.

Unaware of what was going through his mind, Amelie read the note and exclaimed, 'Oh, dear! Dr Balfour and his family have been while I was out.'

'Don't concern yourself,' he advised. 'I spoke to him this morning and he said he'll call again if he misses you, but for now, Amelie, would you like me to stay for a while or would you prefer me to leave?'

For the first time he saw the sparkle of tears in the blue eyes looking into his, but her voice was steady enough as she replied, 'I will be all right, thank you. You helped me through a bad moment and I am grateful, but I am sure that you have other things to do.'

As relief washed over him at being let off the hook he said, 'All right, if that is what you would prefer, but I'll leave you my mobile number just in case.'

'There is no need,' she protested. 'I will be fine once this day is over,' and wished she hadn't been so quick to tell him the reason for her distress. She'd kept the hurt under wraps ever since the break-up with Antoine and would still have been doing so if she hadn't come across a village wedding.

Leo's relief at her insistence that she would be all right was short-lived. While he was out dining with Georgina from the boutique and other friends that evening he was on edge, knowing that he shouldn't have been so quick to latch onto Amelie's reassurances.

The day she'd been dreading wasn't over yet and the hurts that life was prone to hand out always seemed to multiply with the coming of the night.

It was as he'd said. She was alone in a foreign land and although he hardly knew her, he did have some degree of responsibility towards her because she was joining the practice on Monday morning and they would be meeting again. On a different level.

The folks he was with were aware of his wandering thoughts and Georgina asked, 'What's the matter, Leo? Aren't we entertaining enough for you tonight?'

He smiled and there wasn't a woman there who didn't wish he belonged to her, including Georgina, but she was aware that Leo was not the marrying kind, not where she was concerned anyway.

'I have got something on my mind,' he confessed. 'I'm sorry if I'm poor company.' He sent an apologetic glance in Georgina's direction. 'I need to pop out for a while. If I'm not back when you're ready to order, you know what I like to eat, Georgina.' And before anyone could comment he'd gone, striding out of the restaurant with a haste that didn't go unnoticed.

Ten minutes and once again he was outside the

house where Amelie was staying, and when he saw that it was in darkness he was about to turn away when her voice came from behind him.

'Dr Fenchurch!' she exclaimed. 'I wasn't expecting to see you again today.'

'I just came to check that you're all right,' he said smoothly, as if he hadn't been fidgeting on her behalf for the last hour. 'I'm dining with friends in a restaurant not far from here so thought I'd call to make sure.'

'That is very kind of you and makes me even more sorry that I unloaded my troubles on to you,' she told him. 'But concern yourself no longer. I am fine. I beg you go back to your friends and remember you did give me your mobile number.' *Which I am not going to use, no matter what.*

'I shall have an early night to make up for my exhaustion of yesterday,' and as he made no move to take the hint, she said, 'Goodnight to you, Dr Fenchurch.'

He nodded. 'Goodnight to you too, Amelie.'

At which she opened the door and disappeared from sight and he drove back to where Georgina and the others were waiting.

'So who was the woman?' someone asked jokingly.

He sighed and surprised them by saying, 'Her name is Amelie Benoir. She's the French doctor who is joining the practice for a few months. I only met her yesterday and I'm concerned that she is on her own in a strange place where she knows no one except me because Harry asked me to go to the airport to meet her last night. Does that satisfy your curiosity?' he questioned mildly.

'Yes,' the joker said laughingly, 'and we'll all be sure to ask for Dr Benoir when we're sick.'

As he listened to the friendly banter Amelie's face came to mind, framed by a glossy black bob, with a snub nose and wide mouth. So anyone who wanted glamour and the trappings that went with it would need to look in Georgina's direction.

It was hard to imagine anyone not being keen to marry the boutique owner *except himself,* and if anyone should ever ask him why, the answer would be that he couldn't see her as the mother of any children he might have.

In what seemed like another life he'd wanted Delphine, sweet and bubbly, to give him young ones when the time came, but it hadn't worked out that way.

They'd met at college, where so many romances began, and had known from the start they'd wanted to be together for always, but his love for her had been rent with an anguish that had ended in despair when she'd been rushed into hospital with a serious undetected heart problem and it had been too late to save her.

The pain he'd felt then had set the pattern for the years to come. It had been something that he never wanted to have to go through again. He was pursued all the time by women and laughed and joked with them, sometimes had the odd fling, but that was it. None of them could bring the kind of joy to his life that Delphine had.

When Amelie had told him that she was all right, it had been partly to reassure him and also because his kindness and concern on her behalf had helped to turn what could have been a ghastly day into a bearable one, and now she was determined that she wasn't going to lie sleepless and fretting about what might have been.

Antoine Lamont had been a junior doctor at the same hospital as herself. When he'd started paying attention to her she'd thought that the quiet, low-key guy, who had often been on the same shift as herself, had seen her as the right kind for him because she was as average as he was.

Gradually they'd drifted into an engagement with the promise of a white wedding on the very day she'd arrived in Devon with her heart set on a new life far away from the hurts of the previous one.

Her surmise that Antoine had chosen her because she had been the least demanding and overpowering of some of the women he'd known had been shattered when she'd called at his apartment unexpectedly one night in the hospital grounds and found him in bed with one of the nurses, a brassy, auburn-haired creature who was anything but average when it came to looks and curves.

It had been the end of her dream of contentment with a man she could love and trust and the beginning of pain and loneliness because of the deceit of it.

He'd tried to make amends, pleading that it had just been a one-off with the nurse, but she hadn't wanted to hear his pleas and subsequently Antoine and the girl he'd been in bed with had left the hospital together, leaving her to face the pitying looks of others as best she could.

Yet deep down Amelie thought she might have had a lucky escape and accepted that maybe she'd been more in love with the idea of getting married than with the man in question. But as she lay beneath the covers in the master bedroom of the big house that she was going to be rattling around in, she knew that the hurt of rejection had still been there when she'd seen the bride arriving at the church for her wedding that day, and it had been the same man who had met her at the airport who'd helped her to cope with it.

So far Leo had only seen her at her worst. On Monday morning she intended that he was going to see her at her best, with the ups and downs of her arrival in Bluebell cove blotted out.

If there was one thing that she never wanted to appear as, it was needy. With her parents always at the other side of the world, she'd had to fend for herself since her early teens and maybe that was why Antoine had seemed like a calm oasis in her often chaotic life, but he'd turned out to be just the opposite, and with that thought in mind she turned her head into the pillow and slept.

* * *

Sunday was uneventful except for a visit from the Balfours, Harry and Phoebe, with their toddler, Marcus. The senior partner asked if she was happy with her living arrangements and said to let him know if she had any problems with regard to that or anything else.

'I'm aware that you've already met Leo,' he said, 'and the rest of the staff will be looking forward to meeting you on Monday morning, Amelie.'

'Yes, I've met Dr Fenchurch,' she replied. 'I feel I may have interrupted his weekend as I seemed to be everywhere he was.' She wondered if the man in question had told his partner at the practice about her unsuccessful attempt at matrimony.

She hoped not, though she hadn't asked him to keep it to himself, but if he had respected her privacy it would be a stick to measure him by and she was already intrigued by him.

The Balfours didn't stay long, but it was time enough for her to discover a couple of things about them: one, that they were deeply in love and both adored the child; and, two, that she liked them and hoped that Dr Balfour would be as pleasant to work for at the practice as he was outside it.

Monday morning saw Amelie poised and ready for action, dressed in a smart white blouse, short black skirt, and with her smooth ebony hair straight and shining around a face that was alight with anticipation.

She'd made up carefully, paying special attention to her eyes, which she felt were the best feature of a nondescript face, and when she stood in front of the mirror in the bedroom she felt that she'd done her best with what nature had given her because there was nothing wrong with her bone structure and the flesh on it, yet when she thought about a certain brassy red-headed nurse with breasts like balloons she did have her doubts.

* * *

Leo was emerging out of the private entrance to the apartments as she appeared on the practice forecourt and strode purposefully towards him, carrying a leather briefcase. She looked different again, dressed smartly as she was, from the dishevelled woman at the airport and the bikini-clad swimmer on the beach.

'Good morning, Dr Fenchurch,' she said as he fell into step beside her. 'It has come. The day I am to be part of your medical centre.'

'Yes, indeed,' he replied as he held open the main door of the surgery for her to go through. 'I hope you won't be disappointed in us.'

She smiled up at him. 'It is more that it should be me who does not disappoint you and Dr Balfour. When you met me at the airport it was what I saw in your expression…disappointment.'

Surely it hadn't been so obvious? he thought. It had been because he'd picked out the wrong woman to be her that the difference had seemed so great.

He didn't deny it. Instead, he said, 'It was very

rude of me if that was how I appeared, and you are certainly proving me wrong so far. I hope that your first day is a good one, Amelie. Harry is already here and waiting to see you in his consulting room.'

'They came to see me yesterday. Dr Balfour and his family were most kind. I wondered if perhaps you had told them about my cancelled wedding.'

For the first time since she'd met him she saw Leo's pleasant manner chill as he told her, 'Certainly not! If Harry and Phoebe were kind, it's only because that is what they're like. I wouldn't dream of discussing what you told me on Saturday with anyone. Your private life is yours alone.' And with the coolness still there he pointed to the door nearest to them, said, 'That's Harry's room,' and disappeared down the corridor in front of them where all the activity seemed to be taking place.

She'd unintentionally insulted him, Amelie thought as she tapped on the door of the senior partner's room. Suddenly the morning wasn't so exciting and challenging. She was just a temp from across the Channel, a bride-to-be who'd ended up on the outside of things.

Somehow she managed to put on a good face for the head of the practice and smiled her pleasure when he told her that she was being provided with a hire car that would be available the next day.

'You'll be in the room next to Leo at the other end of the passage,' he told her, 'and for a time will do the home visits with him until you are familiar with the area.' He shook her hand. 'Welcome aboard, Dr Benoir. I hope you enjoy your time with us.' And that was that.

His phone was ringing so she left him to it and went to introduce herself to the receptionist at the desk opposite, who in turn took her to meet the rest of the staff, who were gathered in the kitchen for what she was to discover was a daily ritual—a mug of tea before surgery commenced.

The first thing she saw was that Leo wasn't

there and wondered if he was still smarting from what she'd said earlier. On her part it had just been innocent curiosity, yet she could understand his annoyance at the inference that he might have repeated what she'd told him to others.

But there was no more time to dwell on that. There were hands to shake, names to remember, and by the time the introductions were over she was feeling more comfortable.

Amongst those present were the two practice nurses, Lucy the elderly one, and Maria, young, pretty and the daughter of the beach lifeguard.

The district nurse, Bethany, only recently appointed, was there too, as well as the cleaner, a pleasant woman who came early and finished early in time to get her children off to school.

As she drank the tea Amelie was still wondering where Leo was and when she moved nearer to the open kitchen door she could hear his voice coming from Dr Balfour's room and he didn't sound happy.

He'd gone outside to get something out of his car and on returning had found that the senior partner had left Amelie to introduce herself to the staff, instead of doing it himself, and his frown had deepened when Harry had said laughingly, 'She wandered off while I was on the phone. Don't fuss. I've told her she's getting the cherry on the cake.'

'And what might that be?' he'd gritted.

'Doing the house calls with you, of course.'

'Really. And how exciting is that not going to be…for her?'

She'd heard everything that was being said except the last two words because Leo had lowered his voice. If she'd felt she'd upset him before, it was twice as bad now. He obviously had no desire to be lumbered with her on his house calls.

He joined them all in the kitchen seconds later and her glance raked his face for signs of how he was feeling now. She was surprised when he had a smile for her and asked, 'Are you all right, Amelie?'

'Yes. I'm fine,' she told him, relieved to see that he was back to his normal manner. 'I have met all the staff, except the manager of the practice, and someone said she will be along shortly.'

'That's Janet. She doesn't start until nine o'clock, but often works later than we do in the evenings. Bethany, the new district nurse, is her daughter.

'They're a good lot. Don't hesitate to ask any of them if you have any problems. Surgery will be starting in a few moments so let me show you where you will be providing health care for the folk in Bluebell Cove.'

'Are you still angry with me?' she asked in a low voice as he opened the door of the smallest consulting room in the practice.

'No, of course not. It was just you thinking I might have discussed your private life with Harry or anyone else that threw me off balance for a moment.'

He was beginning to wish they weren't having this conversation, didn't want to get any closer to this young French doctor who had butted into his weekend and now wanted to see into his thoughts. He'd actually fallen out with Harry over her and that was a first. They usually got on well.

A change of subject was called for and as the surgery was due to open its doors in a matter of minutes, what better way than to explain to her what was going to be required of her on her first morning?

'Harry and I have picked out a few appointments from today's list for you to deal with,' he explained. 'They are mostly women and children. Since Francine left to go back to her homeland we haven't had a woman doctor on the staff, so you can see the advantages of having you here for our female patients, young and old.

'If anything occurs that you haven't dealt with before, Harry and I are here for help and advice. So good luck on your first morning. And now, if you'll excuse me, I must prepare to meet my own patients. After surgery is finished we'll have a coffee and then it will be time for the home visits. You will be able to see a lot more of Bluebell Cove while we're out in the district as the area that the practice covers is both coast and country.'

With that he disappeared into the room next to hers and Amelie was left with the feeling that he was putting up with her on sufferance. What he'd said to Dr Balfour with regard to there being no pleasure in taking her with him on his rounds indicated that, and also there'd been the darkening of his brow when she'd asked him if he'd told the other man about her non-wedding.

He'd been all right about it afterwards, but there were signs that Leo was finding her heavy going, so a low profile was called for.

Her first patients were a harassed mother with a tearful four-year-old who was protesting loudly that she didn't want to see the doctor man. Both were surprised to see that the 'doctor man' was a smiling young member of their own sex who had a way with children, having worked in the paediatric wards of a French hospital.

Within seconds the child had stopped crying and the mother was calming down as she explained why they were there. 'Tiffany has an inflamed throat,' she said, 'and is very fretful. She won't eat and had a raised temperature during the night. It seems normal enough now, but I still felt she should see a doctor.'

'Yes, of course,' Amelie agreed. 'First I must look down the throat to check the degree of the inflammation.' Turning to the small patient, she said gently, 'Will you open your mouth for me, Tiffany, so that I can shine a light inside it?'

Not too keen on the idea, Tiffany clung to her mother and at her most persuasive Amelie said, 'Just one little peep, that is all. Can you do that for me?'

Reassured, the child nodded and opened her mouth and when, as promised, Amelie did a quick examination of her throat she saw there was infection around the tonsils.

'Has Tiffany had an inflamed throat before?' she asked.

Her mother shook her head. 'No, never.'

'Then let us see what a few days' rest and some paracetemol will do. They will help to relieve the soreness and then Tiffany will be more likely to want to eat. Ice cream is good for an inflamed throat too. If you should see pus on the tonsils, send for one of us immediately.

'Her temperature is normal at present,' she announced when she'd checked it, 'but may rise again in the night so be prepared.' She turned to the child. 'You have been a very brave little girl, Tiffany, and you can have some ice cream when you get home.'

'Thank you, Doctor,' her mother said as they were leaving. 'Are you new here? I haven't seen you before.'

Amelie's wide smile embraced them both.

'Yes, I am here from France for a while and am already in love with your village.'

'I have a woman's problem that I've wanted to discuss with someone of my own sex, so you might be seeing me again,' Tiffany's mother said.

'That will be fine whenever you are ready,' Amelie told her, 'and be sure to bring Tiffany back to the surgery if the inflammation persists.'

An expensively dressed elderly woman with an irregular heartbeat came next and was immediately dubious when she saw a fresh face behind the desk and a young one at that.

'I was expecting to see Dr Balfour,' she said haughtily. 'Are you fully qualified?'

'Yes, I am,' Amelie told her pleasantly. 'I have a degree and have been employed in a French hospital for the last two years. I am here to see how general practice works in the UK. So would you oblige me by unbuttoning your cardigan, Mrs…er…' a quick glance at her notes

'…Arbuthnot, as any kind of change in the heart-beat needs immediate attention.'

'Yes, it is a little fast this morning,' she told the patient when she'd listened to it intently. 'Has it happened before?'

'On and off, but not as severe as this,' was the reply.

'And you have seen Dr Balfour on those occasions? There is no mention of it in your records.'

'No. When it has happened before I've ignored it and it has gradually gone away.'

'But not today?'

'No. Not today.'

'Then an ECG is called for. If you will accompany me to the nurses' room it will be done, and whatever the feedback we will find out what, if anything, is wrong with your heart.'

As Esther Arbuthnot got slowly to her feet she said grudgingly, 'They say that a new broom sweeps clean, so maybe being passed to you for my consultation isn't such a bad idea after all. What is your name?'

'Amelie Benoir,' she said as she led the elderly woman towards the ECG facility, where Lucy would perform the test.

The speed with which the results came through had Esther Arbuthnot in a state of amazement that turned to alarm when she was told that there could be a problem with one of the valves of her heart and that there had been evidence of a minor heart attack some time in the past.

'We need to refer you to a cardiologist for further tests,' Amelie told her gently as she observed how the patient's bumptiousness was disappearing fast, yet not so fast that she wasn't already planning ahead.

'There is a top heart surgeon in Bluebell Cove,' Esther informed Amelie. 'His name is Lucas Devereux and he has a private clinic that he runs from his home.'

'He's the consultant I want to see. I can well afford it. He is married to Barbara Balfour's daughter Jenna, who was a practice nurse here until they had their first child. So if you would arrange for me to see him as quickly as possible, I would be obliged.'

'Yes, of course,' she assured her, 'and in the meantime no excessive exertion. Just take it quietly and rest whenever possible. I will be in touch as soon as I have an appointment for you.'

When she'd gone Amelie wondered how many Balfours there were in Bluebell Cove. They had to be related to Harry Balfour, the head of the practice, in some way. At the first opportunity that arose she would ask Leo who this Barbara Balfour was.

CHAPTER THREE

AMELIE'S first morning at the surgery was over and as she waited for Leo's much longer list of patients to come and go before they set out on the home visits she was thinking how much she'd enjoyed her first taste of general practice.

She'd coped with the patients that had been passed to her by the other two doctors without having to consult either of them, and when Leo finally appeared and asked, 'So how was it?' she had a smile for him.

But there was uncertainty behind it and he thought she was unsure of him, still aware that he hadn't liked being questioned as to whether he'd passed on details of her private life to Harry. But she was not to know that though some saw him as lightweight, he cherished his integrity and admired that of others.

'I enjoyed it immensely,' she told him. 'I liked the one-to-oneness of it. In a hospital situation there are sometimes too many fingers in the pie.'

'So, are you ready for an interesting couple of hours visiting the sick and seeing the sights of Bluebell Cove when we've had a coffee?'

'Yes, of course,' she said obediently, and it was there again, a withdrawal of the unaffected easiness that she'd displayed when in his company previously.

Yet as he pulled out onto the coast road she was the first to speak, and it was to ask if Dr Balfour had relations living in Bluebell Cove. She went on to explain that a patient had mentioned someone called Barbara Balfour.

'Yes, he has indeed,' he replied. 'Harry was brought up in this place and when he got his degree came to work at the practice as a junior doctor like you. At that time his aunt, Barbara Balfour, was in charge of the practice and I'm told was a force to be reckoned with, but she had to retire due to ill health. She and her husband live in Four Winds, the large house on the headland.

'Barbara was instrumental in persuading Harry to come back to Bluebell Cove after losing his wife in an accident, and also helped Ethan Lomax with his problems at the same time. The lady in question is a household name here and revered by all who know her, but she is also something of a tartar, even though she isn't in charge any more.'

'And it is her daughter who is married to the heart surgeon?'

'Yes, she was Jenna Balfour before she married Lucas Devereux. So now you can place us all in our slots,' he said whimsically.

'All except you, Dr Fenchurch. You don't seem to have one. All the others appear to have roots in Bluebell Cove but not you. Where do you come from?'

'The north-west. I'm from Manchester.'

'So you are a long way from home.'

'Yes, but not as far from home as you are, though you seem contented enough.'

She shook her head. 'Not always, I'm afraid. Yet I know I'm going to be happy here, I can feel it inside. Bluebell Cove is so beautiful, how could I not be?'

He gave her a quick sideways glance and thought how different she was from other women he'd known. She had no airs and graces. She was just herself, an enthusiastic young doctor with, from the sound of it, parents who had put their careers before their daughter. Had they been around when in the not so distant past she had suffered heartbreak at the hands of some two-timing upstart?

But she was getting on with her life with an ingenious kind of acceptance that a lot of the women who sought him out wouldn't be able to boast.

'Our first call of the day is at the marine museum next to the harbour,' he said, bringing his thoughts back to the reason they were driving in that direction. 'The caretaker and his wife live in an apartment on the premises and they've asked for a home visit.'

'Why?' she asked, all eagerness on her first venture on house calls with him.

'I'm not sure. It was his wife who rang up and the message was rather garbled. If I understood it rightly, her husband is having some sort of severe gastric attack.'

'Oh, dear, that sort of thing can be most unpleasant,' she commented, and he tried not to smile. If they didn't come across something worse than that during the next couple of hours he would be surprised, but had to have a rethink when he saw the elderly caretaker.

He was deathly white and in a lot of pain, which his wife said had started in a milder way around and above the navel then had increased sharply and was now located at the lower right-hand side of the stomach. When he'd examined the patient Leo turned to Amelie, who had been watching intently.

'Would you like to examine our patient and give an opinion?' he asked, and turned to the man's wife. 'Dr Benoir is going to be working with us at the surgery for a while. She has come over from France to join us.'

Amelie was already doing as he'd requested and when she'd finished she straightened up, looked him in the eye and said, 'I suspect appendicitis.'

'I would agree,' Leo told her. 'The hospital will do a laparotomy and if that is what it shows, they will remove the appendix.'

He was quick to reassure the caretaker's wife. 'I'm sending for an ambulance and if it should turn out to be appendicitis your husband will be operated on without delay to avoid infection spreading.'

'You seem to be something of an expert in diagnosing appendicitis, Dr Benoir!' he commented, impressed by Amelie's confident diagnosis.

'I have seen it in a child. It was in the same place and very painful.'

'So you know that the most dangerous time with appendicitis is when the pain goes. It is the calm before the storm when the appendix bursts and peritonitis develops, so watch out for that.'

When the ambulance had come and gone, with the suffering caretaker and his wife on board, Leo drove them to the next house call, where they found a small boy with measles.

He had a high temperature, the usual rash, and was waiting for their visit in a darkened room as the illness made the small patient very sensitive to light.

'It was wise of you not to bring your boy to the surgery,' Leo told his mother. 'Measles is very infectious. Also I see that you are taking care of his eyes, which is good. Measles is a serious illness that was almost stamped out until the scare that the vaccine might be connected with autism. Am I to take it that your son hasn't had the three-in-one MMR?'

She nodded glumly. 'My husband and I did what we thought was best for him, but now I'm not so sure and am not going to leave his side for a moment until he's better.'

'Plenty of rest and lots to drink will help, and once the rash has gone you will see an improvement. He should stay in quarantine for at least four days so he doesn't infect anyone. Like all the familiar childhood illnesses measles will take its course and the young ones need plenty of care and love while it is doing so.'

As they were leaving the house Leo said wryly, 'Being a good parent is the job of a lifetime and not everyone gets it right or even wants to, but that child's mother was giving it a good try, even though she'd decided on the wrong course of action.'

The moment he'd made the comment about families he wished he hadn't. Amelie's family life didn't sound fantastic, if it existed at all.

When he glanced across she was staring out of the car window, her face expressionless. He hoped he hadn't spoilt her first foray into the world of those not well enough to go to the surgery.

As they made their way back to the practice, once they'd completed all the home visits, Amelie's gaze was fixed on the sea below and suddenly she wound the window down and said urgently, 'The tide is coming in fast around the entrance to a cave down there and I can see children inside.'

He slammed the brakes on and flung wide the door and they ran side by side down the cliff path that led to the beach.

'Where is everyone?' he cried. 'There isn't anyone in sight.'

Waves were crashing against rocks and they could see two small girls crouching in the entrance to the cave, about to be swept out and battered against them any second.

There was no time for discussion between the

two of them. Every moment was vital if they were to get to the children and bring them to safety, but this young doctor was in his charge, Leo thought frantically. If anything happened to her...

He was cold with horror at the thought as he clambered over the rocks and prepared to lower himself into the sea, with her close behind. Calling over his shoulder, he told her, 'I'll deal with this. Stay where you are, Amelie.'

It was too late. She'd run to a point farther along and was already striking out towards the cave and the children trapped there. A powerful swimmer himself, he saw once again that she was in a class of her own in the water.

As they reached the cave a huge wave swept into the opening and on receding brought the children with it. Amelie grabbed one of them, he took the second in his grip and they fought their way to the nearest rocks where they heaved them up to safety as two lots of frantic parents scrambled towards them.

'We only left them for a short time,' one of the mothers cried as she hugged her child to her. 'The men wanted a drink and persuaded us to go with them. The tide was way out then and the children *are* having swimming lessons.'

'The sea came in from the side and was in front of the cave where they were playing before they had a chance to escape,' he explained grimly, 'and it would have been too powerful for children as young as these to swim in a high tide such as this.'

'Yes, well, thanks,' one of the fathers said sheepishly. 'We'll know next time.' And with the children wrapped in towels, they moved towards the car park.

When they'd gone Amelie looked down at her soaking-wet blouse and skirt. Thankfully she'd kicked off her shoes in the car so at least they would be dry.

Beside her, Leo was stripping off his shirt and squeezing water out of his trousers, and when their glances met he said tightly, 'I suppose you didn't hear me when I called that I would handle it. I was having nightmares out there in case something happened to you while you were under my supervision.'

'Is that all you were concerned about?' she asked miserably, as the feeling that she was of no consequence to anyone surfaced once more. 'Concerned that I didn't embarrass you by drowning while I was in your charge? Had you forgotten that I can swim like the best of them?

'When I was young my parents had to take me with them on their postings abroad and often there was nothing else for me to do except go to whatever school was available and spend the rest of my time swimming. I even trained as a lifeguard one summer.'

It had been his turn to offend her, Leo was thinking, but it was no time for soul-searching. She was beginning to shiver in her wet clothes and he said, 'There is a long raincoat of mine on the back seat of the car. Take your wet things off and put it on before you catch a chill. I'll wait here until you've done that and then we'll be off. The village is only a short drive away and you'll be able to have a shower and a hot drink before the afternoon surgery starts.'

She nodded meekly and went to do as he'd suggested. Within minutes they were pulling up in front of the Lomax house and he was bidding her goodbye as he went to change his own clothes before returning to the practice.

Typically of village life, by the time they both arrived back at the surgery Harry and the rest of he staff had heard about their rescue in the cove and he'd opened a couple of bottles of wine for the staff to toast them, which Amelie felt was a more celebratory attitude than Leo's had been. Yet she supposed it was understandable. She might have felt the same in his position, so she could see his point of view.

That she could always see the other person's point of view was her Achilles' heel. She'd even seen Antoine's when he'd opted for someone more raunchy and lively than her. Had known she'd been wrong in thinking that because he was so ordinary and undemanding he would want her, who was the same, when all the time he'd had other ideas.

It hadn't made the hurt any less but she'd understood better and would be very careful in her next choice, if there was ever a next time.

At the end of the day Leo said, 'I'd like a word in private. Would it be all right if I popped across when I've finished here?'

'Er...yes,' she said, with bluebell eyes wide and questioning, 'but only if you aren't going to tell me off again.'

He sighed. 'I'm not going to do anything of the kind. I've got one more patient to see so should be about fifteen to twenty minutes. The guy has phoned to say that he's held up in traffic, so I'll come over when he's been, OK?'

'Yes. I'll be doing steak and salad. Shall I do it for two so that you don't have to cook when you get in, or are you dining out with friends?'

she asked, and couldn't believe what she was saying.

He gave her a long level look and informed her, 'I don't eat out all the time, you know. It's usually weekends when I do my socialising so, yes, thanks for the offer, Amelie. It will be a change from an endless round of ready meals.' *And a change from the kind of company I usually keep,* he thought, *which is long overdue.*

When he came he'd changed again for the second time and was dressed in a smart casual top and jeans, and Amelie thought how incredible he looked with his golden fairness and the trim six feet of him.

Without giving serious thought to how it might sound, she said, 'When you met me at the airport I was half-asleep and thought you were either the Angel Gabriel or some Greek god who had come back to haunt womankind.'

'Really?' he said dryly, with lips pursed and eyes rolling heavenwards. 'I lay no claim to my looks. I inherited them from my Nordic grandfather and in any case what we look like from the outside isn't always an indication of what goes on within.'

'What did *you* think when you saw me?' she wanted to know.

He was smiling and it took the sting out of what he was about to say.

'I thought you were odd, a bit scruffy and rather vacant.'

She laughed at the description. 'I can't deny any of that. I'd just worked twenty-four hours non-stop, had had the quickest shower of my life and flung myself into a taxi, praying all the time that I wouldn't miss my flight. They were calling it as I rushed into the airport and I made it with only seconds to spare, so must admit that my appearance was the last thing on my mind.'

He nodded. 'Yes. That was understandable.'

'And so are you going to tell me why you are here before I serve the meal? I won't be able to eat with curiosity gnawing at me.'

'I came to apologise for my tactless comments

after we'd brought those youngsters to safety. You were incredible, so fast thinking and even faster in the water. Yet even though we were back on dry land with everyone safe and sound I was still imagining what it would have been like if I'd had to tell Harry that you'd drowned on your first day in the practice. I'm sure you can understand that.'

'Yes, I can,' she said soberly. 'I have this bad habit of always being able to see someone else's point of view. Though at that moment it wasn't working too well as you were making me feel that I didn't matter as a person, that I was just an encumbrance, the gauche, wet-behind-the-ears trainee that you'd been burdened with and wanted to take back to the practice intact for your own reputation.'

Stopping for breath, she wondered if she was suffering from some kind of verbal override. She'd hardly stopped talking since he'd appeared and supposed one reason might be that she was nervous in his company.

It was his turn to be amused. 'Thanks a bunch for that powerful description of your opinion of me. If I remember rightly, at the time you were wet in other parts of the anatomy besides the ears, and I'm not too sure about the gauche label. I'd give it five out of ten.'

'Now you're making fun of me.'

'Not at all. I have to say that whatever else you are…you're different. But getting back to why I came, do you accept my apology?'

'Yes, of course. And I thought what *you* did was pretty special too.' Before she said or did anything else that might be misconstrued, she added, 'If you will excuse me for a moment, I'm going to serve.' She indicated the dining room where the table was set. 'If you would like to take a seat.'

Watch it, he told himself when she'd gone into the kitchen. Don't let it get out of hand with this young doctor. She's sweet and caring but not in your league, Leo. She would soon tire of your sort of lifestyle. You aren't over the moon with it yourself these days, especially when you observe Harry and Phoebe. Yet there is something to be said for freedom.

They chatted about everything but themselves while they were eating—the practice, the village, the community and the social life of the place. Amelie listened intently as he described the events that were arranged during the various seasons.

When she discovered that in July there was to be what was known as the Big Summer Picnic, where everyone who went took food with them, either sweet or savoury, to be shared at long wooden tables covered with white cloths, she was already wondering what to wear.

'You haven't said where the picnic takes place,' she reminded him.

'On the field at the back of the village hall. That way there is somewhere to scatter if it should rain, and in the evening there is a barn dance.'

'Do you go to these events?' she asked.

'Yes, usually. It depends on what is going on in my life at the time.' She wondered if that was significant or just a casual comment.

'That was lovely,' he said when they'd finished eating and she'd served coffee in the spacious sitting room. 'Maybe you'll let me do the same for you one evening in my sparse accommodation.

'I stayed at Mariner's Moorings, the guest house on the coast road, for a long time before I moved into the apartment and I've no thoughts of buying a property at the moment. I don't like to be tied down.'

Her expression was downcast as she told him, 'We have different ideas about that. My life has been like that of a Gypsy, lacking stability, especially when I was young, which I feel had something to do with my disastrous broken engagement and cancelled wedding. I thought marrying Antoine would give me security and was mistaken, so it will be a long time before I fall into that pit again.'

'You don't exactly sound as if you were head over heels in love,' Leo commented dryly. 'People *are* supposed to marry for love, you know.'

He was getting to his feet and glancing at the clock with the feeling that it was all getting a bit too intimate. They'd only known each other a few days. He'd been there for Amelie at the start. She should be able to cope from now on.

She was observing him questioningly and he said, 'Thanks for the meal and the hospitality, Amelie, Not having to do the cooking myself will give me more time to get up to date with a lot of medical info that's coming through and waiting to be absorbed. I'll pass it on to you when I've finished with it. Harry has already seen it.'

'That would be great, thank you,' she told him primly, and thought that he wasn't exactly lingering. Yet had she expected him to and, more importantly, had she wanted him to?

When he'd gone striding off across the few

yards that separated the apartment and the large detached house, Amelie went to sit in the back garden beneath a sun still high in the sky, and began to go over in her mind what each of them had said. By the time she'd finished she couldn't believe that she'd been so up front about her life with a stranger.

But Leo didn't feel like a stranger. The things they wanted from life were poles apart, but it didn't prevent her from relaxing in his presence, and as she was only going to be working in Bluebell Cove for a few months, did any of it matter?

It was the end of her first week in the village and already Amelie had established a routine that began with a six-o'clock swim down in the cove each morning before the day got under way,

The beach was usually deserted at that time, apart from maybe a lone surfer. There was just the noise of the tide pounding in and the screeching of gulls overhead to break the silence.

On the third morning of that first week the lone surfer had turned out to be Leo, and when she'd appeared he'd come out of the waves carrying his board and watched her approach.

'Is this a regular thing for you?' he'd asked as they'd drawn level.

It was the first conversation they'd had that wasn't about work since Monday night, when he'd left rather abruptly. Even when there was just the two of them in the intimacy of the car while on house calls, they'd only talked about the two Ps—practice and patient—as if they were each wary of the other. So Amelie had been careful of what she'd said, even though the question he'd asked had been innocent enough.

'Yes, I've been coming down each morning at this time because it's so peaceful. It puts me right for the day. What about you? I suppose there is no novelty in having the sea so close for those who live here all the time.'

He had smiled. 'Of of course there is! I never cease to marvel at the view when I arrive at the headland. Harry was away from here for five years and Ethan has gone for good, but I don't want to leave Bluebell Cove ever.'

'Neither do I,' she'd said with unconscious wistfulness.

'Maybe we won't want you to when your time is up. Have you thought of that? You've only been with us a short time but Harry and I are already impressed with your medical knowledge and general aptitude.'

As he watched her face light up with pleasure he was once again aware of the lack of guile of the young doctor from across the Channel who had even been ready with a good word for the guy who'd hurt and embarrassed her in the worst possible way.

Ignoring his vow to keep it cool between them, he said, 'How are you fixed for coming across to my place one evening? If you remember, I promised to return your hospitality.'

Her cheeks were stained with warm colour and her eyes wide as she told him, 'You don't have to do that. I'm sure you have better things to spend your time on than entertaining me.'

'Why not let me be judge of that?' he replied. 'So when would you like to come?'

'Whenever you say. All my evenings are free as I don't know anyone to socialise with.'

'Shall we say Friday night?' he suggested. 'We will drink a toast to the end of your first week in the practice.'

'That would be lovely.' She glowed. 'Thank you for inviting me...Leo. Is it all right if I call you by your first name when we're off duty?'

'Yes, I was beginning to wonder when you were going to drop the formalities.'

At that point she was throwing off the wrap she was wearing over her bikini and he felt his blood warming as he admired the smooth perfection of her body where everything was in such delightful proportion.

As if she'd sensed it, Amelie had kicked off her sandals and was running towards the sea. When she glanced over her shoulder she saw that Leo had thrown down the surfboard and was following her into the oncoming tide. As they swam together they were just two people enjoying themselves early on a spring morning.

Yet not for as long as they would have liked as not far away there was a waiting room that would soon be full of the people they had been trained to serve, and as they walked back to their respective dwelling places each was wishing they knew what the other was thinking.

But by the time Friday night arrived Amelie had forgotten their easy camaraderie on the beach. She was nervous.

She felt instinctively that she wasn't the kind of woman Leo would want to spend time with. He must have made the gesture out of politeness. How embarrassing *that* was going to be, especially if she had the verbal complaint again and gabbled all the time about something and nothing.

'Stop worrying,' she told her image in the mirror when she was ready to walk across to

Leo's flat. Her ebony bob hadn't a hair out of place and the dress she was wearing always made her feel good because of its cut and colour. But she was still nervous at the thought of dining with the 'Angel Gabriel' again.

The windows of the apartment were wide open. She could hear music and laughter coming from above and hesitated. Leo hadn't said anything about anyone else being there.

When they'd made the arrangement on the beach she'd taken it for granted that it would be just the two of them, but it didn't sound like that. Had he invited some people round because she'd said she didn't know anyone to socialise with?

If that was the case, he should have warned her. There was no way she wanted to be an exhibit in front of a group of his friends. She turned quickly, went back to where she'd come from, and couldn't get the key in the lock fast enough.

It was an hour later when the doorbell rang and she got slowly to her feet, prepared to offer what now seemed like a weak excuse for not turning up for the meal that Leo had invited her to.

'So why didn't you come?' he asked unsmilingly. 'The food is spoiling.'

I'm sorry,' she said weakly. 'I was about to press the buzzer to your apartment when I heard what sounded like a party up above, and I couldn't face a lot of strangers at short notice. Why didn't you tell me you were having friends round so that I might have been prepared?'

He was frowning. 'I didn't tell you because I wasn't, that's why.'

'But I heard the voices and the music.'

'Yes, you probably did,' he commented dryly, 'but being new around here you won't know that there are two apartments. The other one, which Harry used to rent, is occupied by the new district nurse who has replaced Phoebe. She and her family are renting it until they find a house that suits them. They were the ones having the party.'

She listened to what he'd been saying in

complete mortification. 'I am so sorry, but you should have told me. You are right about me not knowing about the other apartment. I remembered telling you I had no one to socialise with and thought you were doing something about it when I heard what was going on up above. But when it came to joining in the fun I could not face a room full of strangers.'

He sighed. 'The only person you would have found there is me, so do you want to come and risk my dried-up offerings, or put it down to experience?'

'I want to come,' she said immediately. 'If there is any excuse for the way I behaved it is that I haven't done any socialising since breaking up with the man who betrayed me. It took away a lot of my confidence in myself, but it is returning, and coming to Bluebell Cove is the best thing I've ever done, Leo.'

He was smiling again. 'So come on, then. The burnt offerings await us.'

CHAPTER FOUR

WHEN he'd invited Amelie to the apartment for a meal that morning on the beach and asked what night would be convenient, she'd said any night and indicated that her social life was non-existent, which was not surprising as she'd only been in Bluebell Cove for a week.

But it had caused him to wonder if it had been a hint. He was the only person she knew, both inside and outside the surgery, and he'd invited her to dine with him. It had been out of politeness and with the feeling of responsibility that had been there ever since he'd brought her to the village. He hoped she wasn't reading anything else into it.

To feel responsible for someone who had joined the practice from choice and who was already proving her worth was ridiculous, he'd thought afterwards. Amelie was no shrinking violet, yet neither was she streetwise and provocative, like some of the members of her sex who sought him out.

As he took her up the wooden staircase leading to the apartments that had been one of the focal points of Phoebe and Harry's romance, he was thinking that all his efforts in the kitchen were going to be well past their best because she'd panicked at the thought of meeting strangers. Yet wasn't that what she needed to do, and wasn't that what *he* was, in spite of them being forever in each other's company since she'd arrived...a stranger?

When he'd shown her into the apartment the first thing he did was check on the state of the hot dishes he'd prepared and left on a very low oven setting. They seemed to have survived and with his concerns about the role in which Amelie might be seeing him put to one side, he gave himself up to enjoying her company.

* * *

The evening that had started badly became an enjoyable occasion as Amelie relaxed into the situation.

She said how much she'd enjoyed the meal, having already decided that she would have eaten it even if it had been burnt to a crisp, but there'd been no need to do that. His cooking was better than hers, and the food hadn't been spoilt while she'd been dithering in the house across the way.

Over coffee they chatted about the hospital where she'd been based since getting her degree, and Leo told her so much about Manchester that she was keen to visit if the opportunity arose.

She was just as interested in anything connected with his life as he was in hers. Where she'd been nervous of spending time alone with him she was now relaxed and ready to talk. But remembering the last occasion when they'd dined together and she'd been verbal non-stop, she was wary of saying too much.

He thought the red linen dress she was wearing was a perfect foil for the raven's-wing colour of her hair, unaware that it was one of a scant selection in her wardrobe that was all the salary of a junior doctor allowed.

Having been with her the previous Saturday, when she'd come across a wedding in the village on the same day that it should have been hers, he wondered what sort of a dress she would have been wearing if it had come to pass, and felt a strange sort of protectiveness at the thought of her generosity in making allowances for her two-timing ex-fiancé's behaviour.

The door of the second bedroom was ajar while she was helping him to clear up after the meal, and the cot that Phoebe's little one had used while they had been living there was on view.

'That is from the time when Phoebe lived here,' he said laughingly. 'I'm not keeping it just in case. I like to be a free spirit and have no plans along those lines at present.'

She didn't join in the laughter. Instead she said,

'Neither have I. It will be a long time before I take any chances on love again. To feel unwanted is an awful experience.'

He didn't take her up on that or it would be there again, the compassion she aroused in him, which was crazy when he considered how long they'd known each other. But there was a simple dignity in the way she'd described her past and present life to him that pulled at his heartstrings.

When they went back into the sitting room Leo said whimsically, 'As you can see, my place is far less salubrious than yours. Phoebe managed to get around to painting the ceiling while she was resident here, but I feel that once she'd met Harry there were far more exciting things to do than decorating. So I'm going to remedy that the first chance I get, and when you come again you will see a big difference.'

So there was a chance she might be here again some time. Concealing her pleasure at the thought, Amelie went to the window and looked out into the night. The light was fading and a

June moon shone like a great silver ball over the headland.

For the first time since she'd arrived at the apartment she let her mouth race ahead of her mind and said, 'Why don't we go for a swim in the moonlight, Leo?'

There was silence and she felt colour rise in her cheeks. He'd asked her round for a meal, not to go down to the beach.

He had come to stand beside her and into the silence that had followed the suggestion said, 'Yes, why not? I've done it before, and no doubt will do it again. It's a fantastic feeling. If you pop across and change into your swimming gear, I'll do the same and will meet you out at the front in ten minutes, OK?'

When they met up again he was carrying a beach bag containing a bottle of wine and two glasses, and with her thoughts still out of control she said, 'You are doing this because you're feeling sorry for me, aren't you?'

'Er, no,' he replied. 'I'm doing it because

watching you in the water is something not to be missed, and it has given me an idea.'

'What do you mean?'

'Ronnie the lifeguard was saying the other day that he needed some help in the evenings, that the guy who shares the job with him is on long-term sick leave and the council is dragging its feet at finding a replacement. He said that just a couple of hours in the evenings would be much appreciated. At this time of year it's the busi-est part of the day down there when folks have finished work and are ready to relax.

'Does the idea appeal to you? I'm sure there would be no problem with the authorities, as long as you were able to do a quick lifeguard refresher course. It would give them time to find someone permanent and it would help Ronnie, who is the father of Maria the young nurse at the surgery.'

Amelie didn't reply immediately. The idea ap-pealed to her immensely, yet what she felt was behind it didn't. Leo had taken note of her comment about her evenings being empty, and to get himself off the hook had come up with an idea that could solve the problem. If she was down on the beach in the evenings as a lifeguard, she wouldn't be hoping that he would fill the gap.

But why should he? The man striding along beside her past the headland and down the steps that led to the cove where the last stragglers were beginning to wind their way upwards must have lots more interesting things to do with his kind of looks and personality.

'I wouldn't mind giving it a try if the authorities will allow it,' she said in a voice that told him she thought she'd read his mind. *So what if she did?*

Amelie had no idea how much she was getting to him with her uncomplicated outlook on life and absence of coquettishness.

He felt sure the powers that be would agree to the idea, and he knew Ronnie would when he saw her perform. If he and they knew she'd been involved in rescuing the two young girls from the sea cave just a few days ago, he imagined they would jump at the chance of a temporary replacement. If Amelie was serious about what she'd said, he would start the ball rolling on Monday.

Not a lot moved in local government on Saturdays.

The tide was coming in less vigorously than it sometimes did and as they swam in its unaccustomed gentleness, with moonlight throwing shadows on the rocks and the sand that the sea hadn't yet reached, there was a tranquillity that they could both feel.

Amelie was so entranced by the magic of the evening that she fantasised about her role as temporary lifeguard leading to a permanent position if they didn't require her any more at the practice when her time was up. It would be one way of staying in Bluebell Cove, something she was increasingly keen to do, still saving lives but in a different way than at present.

They'd come out of the water, and were sitting

on the rocks, idly watching the waves skipping over the sand towards them when Leo said, 'You being a doctor would fit in with the lifeguard role very nicely. Immediate medical assistance on the spot if needed, much better than simply having the required First Aid certificate.'

'Yes,' she said slowly, and almost told him he didn't have to sell her the idea. She was already sold on it. Sun, sea and sand were her life's blood. If at the same time as working at the practice she could put her abilities regarding those things to good use, why not?

The only problem was it being weekend tomorrow. It would be Monday before Leo could speak to anyone, and Saturday and Sunday loomed ahead as empty days.

'Why don't you come down here to have a word with Ronnie over the weekend?' Leo said, picking up on her thoughts. 'It would give you the chance to get to know him and find out what would be required of you in the evenings if the authorities are interested in employing you as a temporary lifeguard. He's a likeable guy.'

'Yes, I suppose I could do that,' she agreed.

It was almost as if he could read her mind. Though did he read it as far as realising that his eagerness to keep her occupied was beginning to show, was it another taste of the unwanted feeling that was bitter in her mouth?

If so, he ought to tell her. It was to be expected that Leo was living a full and happy life before she'd come on the scene, so it was to his credit that he was putting it on hold because he felt responsible for her.

But *she* didn't want it to be like that, just as much as she felt *he* didn't. She'd coped on her own for as long as she could remember, except for the short time that Antoine had been part of her life.

'Shall we go?' she asked flatly, as if the moon's light on sea and shore and the rugged cliffs behind them wasn't enough.

'Why the sudden drop in spirits?' Leo asked,

as if he didn't know. 'Shall we forget the idea of the beach patrol, Amelie? It was only a thought.'

'No, of course not!' she protested. 'It was kind of you to suggest it. I will come down here tomorrow and introduce myself to Ronnie.' Then it happened again, the words were out before she could stop them. 'What plans have *you* made for the weekend?'

Fortunately a cloud passed over the moon at that moment and he didn't observe her mortification at the intrusion into his life once again. Taken aback for a second by the directness of the question, he replied, 'Tennis tomorrow morning with my friend Naomi, a trip to town in the afternoon, and in the evening out for a meal with friends, maybe moving on to a nightclub later.

'On Sundays I do what chores have to be done, go to the pub for an hour late morning, and maybe drive into the countryside in the afternoon for a Devonshire clotted-cream tea.'

'What is that?' she asked curiously.

'Fresh scones, thick clotted cream that the

county is renowned for and strawberry conserve or jam.'

'It sounds delightful.'

'It is,' he replied, and thought it would be so easy to suggest he call for her on Sunday and take her with him if she would like that, yet he wasn't going to. He had to ease off with the woman beside him, otherwise his well-planned bachelor life, stereotyped as it sometimes was, might fall apart if he veered off in a new direction, and *that* would cause some raised eyebrows amongst those he worked with at the practice.

He knew that Harry thought he was crazy, living the carefree life that he'd always led, but the senior partner was in love and had Phoebe and her child who loved him in return. Soon she would give birth to another little one that would be theirs entirely and his joy would know no bounds.

If he was in a situation like the other man's, he would approach life from a different angle, but he wasn't, and neither was he likely to be while mixing with the 'in crowd'.

The life he'd lived ever since losing Delphine was a defence against ever experiencing that sort of pain and heartbreak again. Even now, with the years having gone by, he still couldn't talk about it, so Harry could only judge him from outward appearances.

He got to his feet and said, 'I suppose we *had* better make tracks or Naomi will be calling for me in the morning and I won't be up.'

As they walked back to the village in the silent night Amelie risked another question about his private life, which she didn't think would offend. 'Does your tennis partner live locally?'

'Yes,' he said easily. 'She returned to Bluebell Cove, where she was brought up, some months ago after a distressing divorce, and we got to know each other at the tennis club.'

'Oh, I see,' she said, and thought what could be more appealing than an attractive blonde divorcee? Certainly not a nondescript junior doctor who couldn't even keep Antoine the un-adventurous happy.

Their two residences were in sight and Amelie knew she didn't want this time with Leo to end. Yet end it must, as the next thought that had come to mind was what it would feel like to be kissed by the Angel Gabriel.

When they stopped at her gate it was clear that the man by her side had no such thoughts. His mind was on more mundane things, such as a reminder to lock up securely before she went to bed and a wish for the best of luck with Ronnie down on the beach the next morning.

But she couldn't let him go with just that. Thanks were due because he had given up his evening for her and she said awkwardly, 'I've had a lovely time, Leo. Thank you for the meal and the rest of the evening.' Standing on tiptoe, she brushed her lips lightly against his cheek.

At the moment of contact he stepped back and Amelie felt her colour rise again. When would she ever learn? Antoine's treatment of her should have made it clear that she wasn't ever going to be any man's dream girl. Leo had backed off as if she was infectious, and that was after just a thank-you peck on the cheek. The pleasure of the time they'd spent together was disappearing like water down a drain.

He sensed her hurt. Could tell by her expression that he'd hit a nerve and wanted to kick himself for upsetting her, but Amelie wasn't to know that he was telling himself all the time to cool it with the young French doctor, and a peck on the cheek might soon transfer itself to the lips, and could go on from there.

'You don't have to thank me for *anything,* Amelie,' he said abruptly, to bring an end to the awkward moment that had come out of nowhere. 'It is just a matter of being polite to a stranger who feels out of things because she knows no one here… And now I'm going to say good-night.'

She nodded, and without speaking watched

him move briskly towards the apartments without a backward glance.

'Ugh!' she breathed when she was inside with
the door locked, as Leo had instructed. For
someone known as the village Romeo he had
taken a dim view of that butterfly kiss on the
cheek, which was all it had been. What was the
matter with the man?

Hadn't she made it clear that she wasn't in the
market for love, or any of the trappings that went
with it? And even if she had been, she was way
out of his league, so why had he shied away from
a simple expression of gratitude?

Up in the apartment Leo was also taking stock of
those embarrassing moments outside the house
across the way when Amelie had tried to thank
him and been repulsed.

She wasn't to know how much she'd got
through to him during the evening by just being
there, and how much he'd known it would be a

mistake to let those kinds of feelings take hold. The outcome of it was that it had to stop.

As from Monday morning it was going to be strictly business and nothing else between them. He'd played his part in making her welcome. Now she was on her own, socially and at the practice.

The hire car they'd arranged for her was there, waiting to be used, so he was going to suggest to Harry that she should do some of the house calls on her own, leaving him free of the close contact with her in his car, which couldn't be avoided.

He was as easy with women socially as he was with men, but it was all on the surface. With Amelie it wasn't like that and he knew why. It was as he kept telling himself, she was different, natural, easy to be with, and had a special kind of charm of her own.

With regard to what *she* thought of *him* he'd had a few laughs at the Angel Gabriel description and decided she was way out there. Angelic he was not! Caring and compassionate, yes, maybe, but never that!

The curtains were still drawn at the house across the way when he got up the next morning and he wondered if Amelie really was intending going down to the beach to introduce herself to Ronnie.

When he glanced across again, after having a shower and the leisurely breakfast that was part of the pleasure of Saturdays, the curtains had been opened and he caught a glimpse of Amelie as she passed the surgery in the direction of the beach.

She was dressed for swimming with her suit on under a sarong and was carrying a towel, so was obviously a woman of her word, he thought wryly, and wished he hadn't made the suggestion of her getting to know Ronnie. He had to admit that he liked having her all to himself.

He was already dressed for tennis and had an hour to spare before Naomi was due to call for him. If he put on some speed he might catch Amelie before she got to the beach and persuade her to change her mind.

When he arrived at the headland he saw it was a vain hope. She was already down there, chatting to Ronnie, and there was no way he could intrude.

She looked upwards suddenly and he moved into the shadow of a nearby tree, hoping that she hadn't spotted him skulking up there. She was a pleasure to have around, he thought, but life was becoming more complicated by the minute.

Turning quickly, he headed back to the village and a morning on the tennis courts with Naomi that he wasn't going to enjoy as much as he usually did because each time the ball came over the net Amelie's face would be in the way.

She *had* seen him up on the headland. The white shirt and shorts he was wearing had made him stand out amongst the rocks and shrubs above and Amelie thought surely Leo wasn't so keen to get her off his back that he'd come to check that she was following through their discussion of the night before and having a word with Ronnie?

He was gone in a flash, most likely watching the time for his game of tennis, and she thought sombrely that he need have no further concerns on her behalf. The message had come over loud and clear the night before and no way was he going to see sight or sound of her out of surgery hours from now on.

In fact, she would go even further than that and ask Dr Balfour if she could start doing her share of house calls on her own as she felt confident enough to do so. If he agreed, the only time she and Leo would be in contact was during the morning and afternoon surgeries when for most of the time they would be closeted with their patients.

Her feelings were a mixture of rejection and annoyance with herself for letting her attraction to Leo blind her to the fact that he was just doing the polite thing by looking after her as he had been doing, but he need exert himself no further.

From now on she would be back to her own coping self, the self that he had yet to see, and after being told by the lifeguard that he would welcome her presence on the beach in the evenings and would speak to the authorities regarding her refresher course, he'd even suggested that she join him this very evening to get a feel for the role.

She'd agreed with the suggestion promptly. It meant that what would have been a lonely weekend wasn't going to be so bad because she would be spending most of the time with her other loves, sun, sand and the never-failing tides.

But what would it be like to be loved by the man she'd only known for such a short time, yet couldn't stop thinking about? The same man who'd made it quite clear the night before that she was just an encumbrance, so *he* wasn't going to look in her direction was he? She wasn't his type.

Still, her spirits were lifting as she walked around at the side of the lifeguard and listened to what Ronnie had to say about the organising of beach patrols and the dangers that were never far away.

There were lots of parents with children milling around and teenage lovelies out to attract young males by pouting in front of cameras, which prompted Ronnie to comment that he had a daughter their age.

'Yes, so I believe,' she told him. 'You are the father of Maria, the young nurse at the surgery, aren't you?'

He nodded. 'That I am. Maria has mentioned you often. So what do you think of Bluebell Cove? I hear Dr Fenchurch has been showing you around.'

'Yes, he has been most kind. As for Bluebell Cove, it's lovely. I would like to live here.'

'So what is there to stop you?'

Instead of answering directly, she replied, 'I don't know anyone here.'

'You soon will,' he assured her. 'Working in the surgery and helping out down here, you'll be known to everyone in no time.'

As they strolled around there was no cause for alarm. Everyone was behaving sensibly, and as Amelie listened to Ronnie describing the job and indicating the danger spots on the part of the coastline that he and his fellow lifeguard were in charge of the day dawdled along.

After his earlier furtive appearance on the headland Leo stayed away from the cove when the tennis was over and made his usual Saturday afternoon trip into the town, but by the time he arrived back in the village he was feeling that he couldn't avoid Amelie any longer.

He told himself it was to make sure she was all right after his rejection of her kiss on his cheek that she'd bestowed upon him, which was true in part, but the main reason was that he just wanted to see her, if only for a short time.

He felt that if only he would let her, she could

bring a different dimension to his life, but the problem was he wasn't ready for it. The way he'd behaved when she'd kissed him had been proof of that.

On Amelie's part, her vulnerability was plain to see, and from the little she'd told him about her life till now it wasn't surprising.

Now she'd come to Bluebell Cove, where he'd found himself taking her under his wing, reluctantly sometimes and at others with great pleasure.

It had to stop. She'd had enough upsets in her life. He didn't want to be responsible for another. Added to that his own past had been far from easy, and the pain of it still clung to him, as did the dread of ever having to go through something like that again, and to avoid it he'd chosen the kind of life he'd been living ever since.

Until now he'd had no doubts about it, but along had come Amelie and everything was changing. He had to call a halt. She knew nothing of *his* past and the reason why he'd never turned to anyone else after losing Delphine.

He had never opened his heart to anyone and did not want to put his burden onto her.

She was the first person his glance rested on when he'd parked the car and was walking down the slipway. She was wearing a scarlet bathing costume that was the same colour as the dress of the night before, and once again the colour made a vivid contrast to her hair and the smooth olive skin of her face.

Ronnie was beside her as they chatted to a group of holidaymakers all in a happy mood. She looked carefree and relaxed amongst them, so much so that he turned on his heel and re-traced his steps back to the car.

Leave well alone, he told himself as he reversed out of the car park.

Amelie didn't get a glimpse of him on that occasion. She was too engrossed with the people she was meeting down below, but Leo wasn't out of her mind, far from it. She'd been longing to see him all day. After him telling her what *he'd* had planned for the weekend, she'd been following him in his various pursuits in her mind, and not having seen him on the causeway she reckoned that he would be somewhere either in the town or on his way back.

Yet what did it matter where he was? He could at least have rung her first thing or called at the house for them to make peace. Though why should he? Leo had explained the night before in no uncertain terms the reason for his presence in her limited social life. So instead of fretting she should be grateful that someone like him had been prepared to take the trouble.

She left the beach in the early evening with a promise from Ronnie that he would be in touch as soon as he'd spoken to the powers that be, and windblown and sun-kissed she decided to have an early night.

That resolve was short-lived when Harry Balfour rang to invite her to supper. 'We usually have a few friends round on Saturday nights,' he said, 'and thought that maybe you would like to join us.'

'Our home, Glades Manor, is about a mile out of the village. If you don't want to walk, the car we've hired for you is on the practice forecourt in readiness for Monday morning and Leo has the keys.'

'I think I would prefer to walk,' she told him, 'and thank you for inviting me, Dr Balfour. I would love to come.'

Having already been told how Leo spent his Saturday evenings, she doubted he would be there, so there shouldn't be any awkwardness to cope with from that direction, and as she showered and dressed for the occasion in the red dress once again, it felt odd.

There hadn't been many days since coming to Bluebell Cove that Leo hadn't been a part of, she thought, and knew that the pleasant and interesting time she'd spent with the lifeguard on the beach, and the unexpected invitation to supper, were not going to make up for it.

CHAPTER FIVE

WALKING towards Phoebe and Harry's house in the warm summer evening was pleasant exercise and when Amelie eventually stood in front of the beautiful old building situated in a green glade that was surrounded by the fertile fields of Devon, it wasn't hard to guess from where the name of Glades Manor came.

As she stopped at the gates, taking in the scene, Phoebe came out to greet her, glowing in the later stages of pregnancy, and as the two women shook hands Amelie said, 'Your house is beautiful, Phoebe.'

'Yes, it is,' she agreed, with a smile for the young French doctor. 'The three of us are so happy here.' She patted her extended waistline. 'And soon there will be four.

'Come inside and meet the others,' she said, leading the way into the house.

Amelie obeyed cautiously, bracing herself for the introductions that must surely follow.

An elderly woman in a wheelchair turned out to be *the* Barbara Balfour, one-time head of the practice and Harry's aunt. The man standing beside her was her husband, Keith. An attractive blonde with a friendly smile was introduced as Jenna, daughter of the elderly couple, and her distinguished-looking husband was Lucas Devereux, the heart surgeon.

Elderly, grey bearded and the last to be introduced of the members of the small supper party was Desmond Somerby, the local Member of Parliament.

With the exception of Barbara Balfour, who was looking her over as if she was something under a microscope, they were all pleasant and friendly towards the newcomer in their midst. There was just one thing stopping her from enjoying herself: Leo wasn't there.

She knew why, of course. He would be somewhere in the town, hitting the night spots with his friends. When Harry had rung her she'd been relieved at the thought of not having the encumbrance label of the night before stuck on her once again, but it had been a long day without him and could be an even longer evening in spite of the good company she was with.

At one point in the evening the doctor who had made the Tides Practice her life's work wheeled herself across to where Amelie was sitting and said, 'They tell me at the surgery that you are doing well so far, Dr Benoir. How do you like our country and our National Health Service?'

Amelie's wide smile flashed out. 'I love everything about it, Dr Balfour, and feel privileged to have the opportunity of being employed in such a lovely place.'

The eyes that had looked her over speculatively when she'd arrived had lost their chill and the woman beside her was smiling as she said, 'That is what I wanted to hear. You have two excellent doctors to call on at the practice if need be, and our womenfolk will be happy to see someone of their own sex available to treat them. I hope that you enjoy your time with us.'

Amelie hadn't heard a car pull up outside because of the chatter inside, but a ring on the doorbell brought a moment's silence as Harry went to see who was there. The voice coming from the hallway was easily recognisable.

'I'm sorry to butt in,' she heard Leo say. 'I've only just seen the email you sent to say that Amelie might need the keys for the hire car to get here tonight. I went out at five o'clock and have only just got back, so I came to make sure that she found you all right and to see that she gets home safely.'

She had listened to what he was saying with a mixture of pleasure and surprise that had overtones of embarrassment as the rest of the guests observed her curiously.

When he appeared in the doorway of the sitting room, his glance went straight to her. Not caring that he had an audience, he said, 'I'm sorry about the car keys, Amelie. What did you do, walk or get a taxi?'

'It was such a beautiful evening I walked here,' she told him as the long day without his presence righted itself.

Phoebe appeared at that moment to call them in to supper, which was being served in the dining room, and with a smile for Leo said, 'You are just in time.'

'That is the best news I've heard today,' he said laughingly. 'I've had a joiner doing some work in the apartment for me. He was using a saw and it slipped and sliced into his hand, so I had to take him to hospital, and we were in A and E for ages, waiting for him to be seen. There'd been a pile-up on the motorway and quite a few casualties had been brought in just before we got there at five o'clock this evening He was seen to eventually, they put sutures in the cut and I've just taken him home.'

His gaze had been on Amelie all the time he'd

been speaking, taking in the glow that a day on the beach had given her and admiring once again the red dress that suited her colouring so much.

He wanted to ask her what Ronnie had said about her helping out as a temporary lifeguard, and if she'd enjoyed her time down there with him. Ronnie was a staunch family man who loved his wife and children and would see that Amelie came to no harm.

Questions like those would have to be asked in the car on the way home, he decided, and made sure that he sat beside her at the supper table, telling himself that it was just in case she was feeling out of her depth amongst strangers.

It was gone midnight and he had her to himself at last, but before he could ask her about her day Amelie had a question for him.

'Why didn't you come down off the headland this morning?' she asked. 'Were you spying on me?'

'Spying? Of course not!' he protested indignantly. 'Checking up on you, yes. I wanted to make sure you were all right after last night, and from where I was standing it seemed that you were, so I went. Does that satisfy you?'

'Yes. I suppose so.'

'You don't sound so sure.'

'Well, last night you made me feel like an encumbrance, yet you are still involved in your unnecessary "duty" of keeping an eye on me, as on the headland this morning, and tonight.'

He sighed. 'What about tonight?'

'You came looking for me to make sure I would get home safely and…'

Her voice was thickening and when he gave her a quick sideways glance he saw the wetness of tears on her cheeks.

'You're crying, Amelie. What have I done now?'

'Nothing,' she sobbed. 'It's just that you are the first person to care a damn about me in ages. I know it's because you feel that you must under the circumstances, me being alone in your country and the rest of it, but you didn't have to, did you, Leo? You could have left me to my own devices.'

Pulling the car up at the side of the road, he took a tissue out of a box in the glove compartment and wiped her eyes gently. As she gazed at him tearfully he reached out and took her in his arms, and as she nestled against him he patted her shoulder and said, 'Shush, don't cry, Amelie. If you keep saying things like that, I'll be getting too big for my boots.'

She was smiling up at him through her tears. 'I don't think the Angel Gabriel ever had that problem.'

'Yes, well, we won't go into that,' he said dryly. 'I've already explained that angelic I am not. Though I must admit that getting to know you is proving to be character building.'

'Now you're laughing at me,' she protested.

'No, I'm not,' he informed her gravely, 'but if I'm supposed to have your welfare at heart,

I ought to be taking you home at the end of a long day, and while I'm doing that you can tell me what Ronnie had to say and if you are still keen on the beach patrol idea.'

He removed his arms from around her and switched on the engine, and as she settled back in her seat she told him, 'He is all for it and is going to speak to someone about getting me re-trained and starting as soon as possible.'

'So you're happy about that?'

'Yes, I am, just as long as you'll come to see me down on the beach sometimes.'

'Of course. It goes without saying, if only to watch you swim.'

When they arrived at the house he saw her safely inside and when she would have asked him to stop for a coffee he forestalled her as he'd done before by saying, 'Make sure you lock up securely, Amelie.'

Pushing caution to one side, she asked, 'When will I see you again?' And he found himself ignoring the vows he'd made not to spend so much time with her.

'You know the Devonshire cream tea that I mentioned as part of my Sunday afternoon routine? How about I pick you up at three o'clock tomorrow and introduce you to yet another of the delights of this part of the world?'

'Yes. I'd love that,' she told him.

'It has to be on a promise, though.'

'What sort of promise?' she asked slowly, coming back down to earth.

'No more tears, Amelie.'

She smiled. 'I think I can promise that.'

The smile was still there as she went upstairs to the big empty bed in the master bedroom of the house. But Leo's expression was more sombre as he went to his own solitary bed. He hadn't wanted to leave her. Had gone against all his promises to himself to cool it with Amelie by arranging to spend time with her tomorrow. The last thing he wanted to do was cause her more heartbreak after her experience with the French guy. He should have had more sense.

But at least he wouldn't be as much in her orbit after tomorrow. On Monday Amelie would be on her own for home visits, and closeted away in her own small consulting room the rest of the time. If she went down to the beach in the evenings she would be fully occupied there, while he would be fretting on the sidelines, wanting her, yet not wanting her, because with commitment could come pain and hurt that knew no bounds. He accepted that what had happened to him and Delphine was likely to occur only in one in a thousand people's lives, but it had done nothing to ease the heartache and loss that had made him what he was now.

When Leo called for Amelie the next afternoon she was ready and waiting, bluebell eyes sparkling with the pleasure of being with him again. Dressed in white leggings and a turquoise casual top that showed off the tan that she was gradually acquiring, he could hardly believe that she was the same bedraggled woman that he'd gone to meet at the airport. It might be simpler if she was, he thought wryly, then he wouldn't be living from one moment of seeing her to the next.

Georgina had phoned earlier to ask why he'd been missing the night before. He'd told her about taking the joiner to hospital and she'd been mildly sympathetic, then changed the subject to a cruise she'd booked and asked if he wished he was going with her.

He'd made no comment but thought there wasn't anything he fancied less than that. Taking Amelie into the countryside was the uppermost thought in his mind and after they'd exchanged a few stilted sentences Georgina had rung off.

He took Amelie to a farm restaurant for afternoon tea, and as he watched her enjoying the food she said, 'I skipped lunch and saved my hunger pangs for this.'

'It would seem so,' he replied whimsically.

Leaning forward, he wiped a blob of cream off the end of her nose with a paper napkin. As she smiled across at him it all seemed so right, the two of them together, light-hearted and in tune on a summer afternoon.

When they'd finished eating he said, 'Do you want to go for a stroll before we go back? There's an old and empty abbey not far from here. It's a tourist attraction now, a beautiful ancient building that brings a lot of visitors.'

She was observing him in surprise. 'I'd love to see it, but are you sure, Leo? I wouldn't have thought it would be your type of thing.'

'Really? And so what *would* you expect it to be? A casino, a club, dining at the Ritz?' he said dryly, and it was clear that he wasn't joking. Before she could reply he went on, 'My looks are the bane of my life. They automatically say party person, and even my profession doesn't totally dispel the image. Sometimes I take the easy way out and just do what is expected of me.'

It might have been a good moment to explain why he lived the kind of life he did, which was a strange mix of dedicated doctor and playboy, but the day had yet to come when he was ready to confess that to anyone, so he told her, 'Yes, I am happy to visit the abbey. Shall we make a move in that direction? I'm not sure what time it closes on Sundays.'

She nodded and with the brightness of the afternoon dimming fell into step beside him. It was clear that her casual remark had hit a nerve where Leo was concerned. She'd better be more careful in future. Yet did she want to have to do that, watch what she said all the time?

When they arrived at the abbey and joined a party being shown around by a guide, he took her hand and said in a low voice, 'Sorry I was snappy. It was directed at life in general, not at you.'

'It's all right,' she told him, vowing to be more careful about what she said around him. Obviously she'd hit a sore spot, and she remembered when in fun she'd mentioned the angel Gabriel comparison, and he'd been quick to point out that the outside appearance of a person was just the shell. It was what was beneath it that mattered.

He was still holding her hand as they admired the stained-glass windows of another age and the empty cloisters that the monks had occupied. When they came out of the shadowed interior into the sunlight he said, 'Old buildings fascinate me. Take Harry's house, for example. It has a charm that modern architecture will never capture.'

She shrugged and there was indifference in the movement. 'My parents own a chateau.'

He was observing her in amazement. 'What? They live in a chateau?'

'Yes, though only rarely. They are away such a lot and are not in residence more than twice a year.'

'And what about you, Amelie? Don't *you* ever stay there?'

'Not if I can help it. The chateau is beautiful from the outside but dusty and damp inside.'

'You amaze me,' he said as they began the walk back to the restaurant to collect the car.

'Why is that?'

'It is difficult to describe. You seem frail, yet you are strong. Have no false pride, and can forgive those who hurt you.'

'Stop!' she cried. 'You are making me into what I am not.'

'So how do *you* see yourself?'

'As a very ordinary person in a beautiful foreign land.'

'I'll bear that in mind,' he said laughingly. 'You are a very ordinary person whose family own a chateau.'

'Yes, that is what I am, and would prefer a house with central heating.'

They were almost home and Leo was about to deliver a body blow. He was going to explain that he hadn't been able to resist spending the afternoon and early evening with her, but now it had to stop because he felt he wasn't being fair in monopolising her, as he had been from the day of her arrival in the village.

It wasn't the truth, of course. If the past wasn't still tugging at him, he would have no reason to back away from her and would 'monopolise' her to his heart's content.

But he'd never overcome the aching void inside him because after Delphine he didn't trust himself to be able to carry through the demands of complete commitment to another woman.

He wasn't sure how Amelie would react when he'd said what he had to say. She was not predictable, but he was soon going to find out. When they pulled up outside her temporary residence he said gravely, 'Can I come in for a moment?'

'Yes, of course,' she said brightly, with the pleasure of the time they'd just spent together coming through in her smile.

'Can I get you a drink?' she asked when they were facing each other in the sitting room.

He shook his head. 'No, thanks. I will say what I have to say and then I'll go.'

Her eyes widened and she said with a shaky laugh, 'That sounds ominous. What is it that I have done?'

You've changed my life, was the reply he would like to have had for her, but it would hardly fit in with what he'd been grimly rehearsing.

He watched the colour drain from her face as he began to speak in what he hoped was a voice of logical calmness. When he'd finished she said with quiet dignity, 'You have just made something that was light-hearted and casual seem as nothing. I have felt sometimes that you found me too much in your face. It was why you suggested I could occupy my evenings down on the beach, wasn't it? As to your comment about monopolising me, I don't hear you asking how I feel about that, if I liked it or not. It's more a matter of you offloading me, isn't it, Leo? I will bear in mind what you have said, and now will you please go.'

He took a step towards her and with her voice rising she said, 'Do not come near me, Leo. All my pleasure at being in your country is due to you and the practice, but mostly to you. Now it has gone and I have done nothing wrong that I am aware of.

'I will not repay Dr Lomax, far away in France, for his kindness by breaking my contract with the Tides surgery. But the moment it is complete I will be gone.'

He had listened in silence to what she had to say, the same as *she* had done while *he* had been saying *his* piece, and now he pointed himself towards the door and did as she'd asked, wanting to kick himself for not telling her about Delphine.

When he'd gone she walked slowly up the stairs and threw herself down on the bed. White-faced and tearless, she gazed up at the ceiling.

You are the unwanted one again, she told herself, and don't blame Leo. He has been merely doing the honours on behalf of the practice and now wants to end it so that he can get on with his own life again, so don't take offence.

Yet this time she didn't feel prepared to turn the other cheek. She'd done no wrong in being attracted to a man who had shown her nothing but kindness and was now wearying of the task he had set himself. The coming Monday morning at the practice was taking on the shape of an ordeal instead of the pleasurable time she'd been looking forward to.

In the apartment across the way Leo's thoughts were no happier.

He'd already suggested to Harry that Amelie should do the easiest of the home visits on her own as from Monday. So when she was informed of the arrangement she was going to see it as a follow-up to today's catastrophic clearing of the air, which would make everything worse between them.

What she'd said kept going through his mind.

That he'd turned a relationship that had been light-hearted and casual into nothing. It had been a bit strong but he'd got the gist of it, and admitted he deserved top marks for the effort he'd put into spoiling it.

He'd even found her an evening job down on the beach to keep them apart, which she'd referred to coldly. Yet he had known he wouldn't be able to keep away from her even then. She was the best thing that had happened to him in years, but because he couldn't forget the past he'd spoilt what they'd had.

She'd already been hurt by lover boy across the Channel, and been cursed with parents who were never there for her. He longed to make up for those things, but whether *he* would ever be the right one for Amelie was another matter.

He wasn't wrong about her reaction when Harry said first thing on Monday morning, 'You are on your own today with the home visits, Amelie. We're passing on to you the ones that should be the least traumatic. Although one can never be sure of that. Some of the calls we receive asking for a visit don't describe clearly enough the seriousness of the problem. Anyway, see how you get on. If you come across anything you can't handle, give one of us a ring.'

She managed a smile that was a cover-up for what she was really thinking, which was that Leo had to be behind her suddenly being seen as ready to work on her own.

As if Harry had read her mind he said, 'Having had you with him while he was doing house calls, Leo feels that you are ready to go solo.'

There had been no sign of him so far and she said casually, 'Where is Leo, Dr Balfour? I haven't seen him since I arrived.'

'Went out on an urgent call at eight o'clock and isn't back yet,' he said briefly, and went to sort out his own day.

By the time Leo returned, Amelie was already dealing with her allocation of those in the waiting room, and as the morning progressed there was no time to dwell on anything but the problems of patients who had come for help and relief from the failings of the body.

Jonah Trelfa was one of those. A strapping sixty-year-old farmer with snow-white hair and a ruddy complexion, he'd come with chest pains and breathlessness, which had set alarm bells ringing.

Amelie had worked in a cardiac unit in the French hospital that she'd left in so much haste to catch her flight to the UK, and knew the signs of a heart problem.

'Is it just indigestion, Doctor?' he asked when she'd finished examining him, almost pleading for a reprieve.

'I don't think so, Mr Trelfa,' she told him gently. 'Your heart is not behaving itself at the present time and needs sorting. If you would like to come with me to the nurses' room they will do an ECG and we'll take it from there.'

The results indicated that atrial fibrillation was present and before she sent for an ambulance

Amelie went to seek out one of the other doctors to confirm that she was doing the right thing.

Harry was with a patient but Leo had just returned from what had turned out to be a lengthy house call, and as their glances met she was relieved that their first meeting after the putdown of Sunday night should be about the needs of someone else rather than their own.

When she'd explained about Jonah's ECG she said, 'Could you spare a moment to examine him first before I summon an ambulance?'

'Yes, of course,' he replied, and when he'd done as she asked said, 'Send Mr Trelfa to the cardiac unit straight away. There are worse heart defects than atrial fibrillation, but no GP should hesitate to send a patient with that kind of problem to be checked out.'

As he turned to go he asked in a low voice, 'Everything all right?'

'Yes. Fine. Just doing my job *and* taking life as it comes,' she told him lightly, then closed the door behind him and gave her attention to

Jonah, who needed her more than Leo did. But the feeling that life in Bluebell Cove had lost its sparkle was still very much in her mind.

She'd been totally content since arriving there with a place in the practice waiting for her, and with Leo, fantastic Leo, kind and supportive all the time. But now he wanted to opt out of their brief enchanted relationship for reasons that *he* understood…and *she* didn't.

By the time Jonah had departed in the ambulance to Hunter's Hill Hospital, exhibiting a stoic calm for someone with newly diagnosed heart disease, Leo was closeted with his own patients and the morning progressed in the Tides Practice until it was time for a quick bite and then off into coast and countryside to visit the sick and suffering. So far the only time they had spoken had been the brief exchange of words about a patient.

That was about to change. When Amelie went out onto the forecourt of the practice to acquaint herself with the car that had been provided for her, Leo was on the point of leaving but stopped when he saw her. Winding down the car window, he asked, 'So are you au fait with the arrangements for today, Amelie?'

'And what arrangements would they be?' she asked coolly.

'Doing the home visits on your own.'

'Yes. I'm "au fait" with most things', she told him. 'I'll phone if there is anything I am not sure of.'

'Of course,' was the reply, 'but we *are* talking about the practice.'

'Exactly,' she agreed, and settled herself behind the wheel of the hire car with a determination that had a message of its own.

Her first call was at the home of a smart middle-aged woman called Beverley McBride, who was much involved in village affairs, but not on this occasion.

A week ago she had been operated on for the removal of her gall bladder by keyhole surgery and of the three incisions made in her chest and stomach, two were healing well, but the third was not.

It had the redness of inflammation with a blueish tinge to it and Amelie prescribed anti-biotics, along with a warning that if there was no improvement in a couple of days to contact the practice immediately.

'I'm surprised you didn't go back to the hos-pital as that is the place where you could have caught the infection,' she said when the patient was ready for off.

'Yes, I know,' Beverley agreed, 'but when I was discharged they said if I had any problems I must see my GP.'

'Fair enough,' Amelie replied, unaware that she would be seeing Beverley McBride again very soon.

Her next call was a routine one at the moment. A daily visit to yet another middle-aged woman who had just had a bone from a bone bank fitted in her hip socket in place of her own, which had crumbled away, and was being given regular injections in the stomach to stop infection at such a delicate stage of her recovery.

It was all very exciting to be working on her own instead of being the onlooker that she'd been when out on the district with Leo, but it didn't take away the hurt she'd been carrying around with her ever since the previous night.

Having accomplished all the visits she'd been given to do, Amelie was driving back to the surgery when she was surprised to see Leo parked at the side of the road in the process of changing a flat tyre. When she would have driven past, he flagged her down.

When they'd separated outside the surgery and he'd driven off in the opposite direction from her, he'd thought so much for last night's diplomacy—a bull in a china shop would have been less clumsy.

He must have been insane to be prepared to cancel out their attraction to each other because of what had happened long ago, but its effect on him was still there in the form of always avoiding any kind of commitment with the opposite sex, and he'd felt that was where they were heading.

He'd never given much thought over the years to what those he met saw him as, had been carefree and popular wherever he'd gone, but had always been on his guard.

Then along had come Amelie, younger than him and on her own due to the selfishness of others. He'd been jolted out of the life he'd led and was having to take a long, hard look at himself.

He supposed meeting her might not have led to so much soul-searching if he hadn't the example of Harry and Phoebe's love for each other always in front of him, along with the other man's comments about what he saw as Leo's empty life, a situation that would have lingered on if he hadn't met Amelie.

So what had he done? He'd called a halt to the wonderful thing that had been happening between them before it had had a chance to take hold because he was discovering that her happiness was very important to him.

For her to be hurt again by him would be unthinkable if he couldn't forget Delphine, so he'd been prepared to end it, hadn't slept a wink afterwards, and the result was she hadn't been prepared to stop on seeing him there by the roadside until he'd waved her down.

He wasn't to know that the desire to pull in beside him had been there but not the certainty that it was the right thing to do after what he'd said the night before, so she would have driven on if he hadn't signalled for her to stop.

When she went to stand beside him in a lay-by at the road edge, with a reluctance that didn't go unobserved, he was almost done and ready to be off, but looking down at his hands, which were decidedly oily, it seemed as if it was the right moment to say, 'I flagged you down to ask if you have any wipes with you to get my hands clean. I usually have some in the glove compartment but must have run out.'

He'd been so desperate to have a moment alone with her that he'd come up with a trite excuse to get her to stop, and as she fished a packed out of her bag and handed it to him he thought that it had been all he could think of at that moment, and hoped that in the near future Amelie would have no reason to look in the place he'd described as being empty of them.

As he wiped the grime off his hands the silence she was hiding behind continued, and wanting to end it he asked, 'So how has it gone, doing the rounds on your own?'

She spoke at last and her voice sounded stiff and formal. 'All right, thank you. Dr Balfour explained it was on your advice that I was doing some of the rounds on my own, and I felt quite sure that it was all part and parcel of last night's dumping.'

'That's an ugly word. I hate it.'

'But you don't hate what it stands for. You'd already put your plans into motion for getting rid of me with regard to our shared visits to the

patients, and followed it up by preaching the
gospel according to you. But as I'm used to the
role of cast-off, it wasn't such a shock. Though
there is one thing that puzzles me, Leo.'

'And what is that?' he asked bleakly.

'You've never made love to me or even kissed
me. So why did you warn me off, unless you
thought the nondescript French doctor at the
surgery might fall in love with you and mess
up your pleasure-loving private life?

'If that *was* the case, you need no longer concern yourself. You are just one of those who have
found me surplus to requirements, so fret not.'
And, wanting to make a statement, she strode
across to her car with a graceful leisured step
until, with her hand almost on the door handle,
she was swung round and found her face only
inches away from his.

'Did you listen to a word I said last night?' he
demanded. 'Or were you so full of your hurt that
it didn't register with you that I was trying to
save you from more of the same kind of thing?

'No, I've never kissed you, or made love to you, and you think it's because I don't want to, do you? Well, how about this for an introduction?' Taking her face between his still oily hands, he kissed her, gently at first, then, as she became aroused, more demandingly, until she was limp in his arms.

It took another motorist pulling up noisily in the lay-by to bring them back to reality. With cheeks bright red and the rest of her weak with longing Amelie moved out of his arms and as they faced each other he said huskily, 'Now do you understand?'

'No!' she told him weakly. 'I don't. How can I?'

Opening the car door, she eased herself into the driver's seat and drove off into the summer afternoon, leaving him standing motionless, as if the last few moments had turned him into stone.

CHAPTER SIX

THE next morning, with all three doctors closeted with their patients in the first surgery of the day, Amelie considered that for anyone else those stolen moments in the lay-by would have been the beginning of a tender, breathtaking romance, but not when she was the woman involved.

Leo had asked her if she understood after setting her senses on fire but there was no way she could have said she did.

It was as if what had just taken place between them had been an ending rather than a beginning. She was bewildered by what was happening to them. Yet one thing had been made clear. Now she knew that given the chance she could love Leo with heart, mind and body, if he ever gave her the opportunity.

He was passionate, mind-blowingly attractive and kind. But there was no way she was going to let those things sweep her into a situation where she was going to be hurt again. Leo had got it right about that. A man with fewer scruples would have led her on, but not him.

It might work for someone else, a tougher woman, less vulnerable than she was, but not for her. If she was on her own for the rest of her life, it would be better than making a mistake now, so she was going to do as Leo had asked and stay away from him in every way except at the practice, where she would try to avoid him as much as possible.

Right now she had to focus on her patients, and she was surprised to see that her next one was Beverly McBride, her gall-bladder patient.

She had given her a supply of antibiotics to clear the infection and now she was back to say that the inflammation was disappearing, but during the night a clear water-like substance had started to come from the wound and it hadn't been just a dribble.

Needless to say, it was causing concern and when she'd examined the source of it and taken note of the much-improved state of the infected area, Amelie asked. 'Did it smell at all?'

The answer was no and she explained that it would be some sort of aftermath of the operation. That sometimes air and fluids are pumped into the area where that kind of surgery was to take place.

'It doesn't always happen,' Amelie told her, 'but I've seen it a few times. It is drainage, which is a good omen rather than a bad one. But on the other hand, if it occurs again I suggest that you ring the hospital just to be sure.'

'They told me not to get in touch with them if I had any problems,' Beverly reminded her.

'Yes, maybe they did, but one thing they *didn't* tell you was that this might happen, so I feel you are entitled to put the ball in their court if they refuse to see you.'

When she'd gone, only partly reassured with instructions to ring the hospital, preferably, or otherwise the surgery if it happened again, Maria, the young practice nurse, came in with coffee. She paused for a second to say, 'My dad thinks you are a fantastic swimmer. He's looking forward to you giving him some help in the evenings down on the beach.'

Amelie smiled across at her from behind the desk and told her, 'I'm looking forward to it as well, Maria.' She added wistfully, 'From what he has told me, it sounds as if you are part of a very happy family.'

'Er, yes, I suppose I am,' she agreed, surprised at the comment but having no cause to disagree. 'Mum and Dad are fantastic. He's great with us kids *and* with those he meets on the beach.'

'Yes, I'm sure he is,' Amelie said with a vision of brief visits to a chilly chateau coming to mind and years of birthday and Christmas gifts sent by mail order.

Breaking into her sombre memories, Maria said, 'Have you seen Dr Fenchurch with the children who are brought to the surgery? He is fantastic too. Has lots of patience, makes them laugh, yet doesn't let a single thing escape him medically. Parents with a sick child nearly always ask to see *him*.'

Amelie swallowed hard. What Maria had said described him exactly. Leo was another man who would make a good father from the sound of it, but he seemed to have doubts about the rest of married life or he would have been spoken for long ago.

It was all becoming just too confusing and when Maria had gone back to the nurses' room she called in her next patient and so the day progressed.

At six-thirty Leo was still ensconced in his consulting room so she made a quick departure and went back to the house for a snack and a change of clothes before going down to the beach to renew her acquaintance with Ronnie the family man once more.

* * *

A short time later, with his day at the practice over now, Leo saw her leave from the window of his apartment and thought that Amelie must feel she had seen and felt enough of him for one day. His presence on the beach this evening would be about as welcome as a rip tide, and, going into his kitchen, he began to make himself a leisurely meal.

A couple of hours had passed and the sun was still high in the sky. He'd been watching for her return and so far it hadn't materialised. He hoped that Ronnie had sorted something out about getting her employed in the proper sense of the word as a temporary lifeguard and not as a voluntary performer. Giving in to the urge to go and find out, he set off for the headland.

When Amelie had arrived there earlier the beach had been packed with families and teenagers enjoying the sun and the sea as white-tipped breakers surged back to where they'd come from, but now the numbers were lessening as folks went to eat in the café at the top of the causeway, in a restaurant in the village or just went back home for whatever was on offer, and he saw her sitting on a rock, gazing out to sea as she ate an ice-cream cornet.

He smiled. Just seeing her again was making him feel better and he went striding down from the headland to join her, not sure of his welcome but chancing it nevertheless, and noting as he did so that there was no sign of Ronnie anywhere.

As if she sensed he was near, Amelie turned and her heartbeat quickened at the sight of the golden man who had captured her heart and was wishing he hadn't. Why was he there? she wondered. To carry on where they'd left off in the lay-by yesterday?

'Hi,' he said when he drew level. 'Where's Ronnie?'

'Gone back home for a well-earned meal.'

'So what sort of arrangement is this going to be?' he questioned. She was so amenable he wasn't going to allow anyone to take advantage of it, himself included.

'He's got permission from the authorities for me to help out in the evenings and at weekends if I so wish. I'm booked onto a refresher course this weekend, so can start immediately after that.'

'And are they going to be paying you for it?'

She was frowning. 'What is all this about, Leo? Yes, I will be paid at the rate for temporary employees, and I'm looking forward to being by the sea and being on hand to help anyone who might need me.

'It must be a wonderful feeling to be needed, though I wouldn't know. I'd begun to think that was all going to change, but I was wrong, wasn't I? Should have known better and taken note of what Lucy and Maria have told me—that you have only to give them a glance and half the women of the village would come running.'

That was one for him, he thought, cringing at the implication, but it was only partly true.

He'd spent a major part of the previous twelve months driving to and from Manchester to look after his mother while at the same time trying to hold on to the position in Bluebell Cove, which he'd only just settled into when she'd become ill. If his sister hadn't come over from abroad and offered to take their mother back with her, he would have had to leave the place that he'd fallen in love with on sight, the same as Amelie had.

Ethan had proved a good friend in those dark days by keeping the position open for him, even though he hadn't been there half the time, and he wasn't ever going to forget that.

Maybe he had gone off the rails a bit when his sister had stepped in. He'd been on a high after months of pressure, but it didn't mean he'd slept around or deliberately gone out of his way to attract the opposite sex. The reason for that had been because he'd never met anyone who could replace Delphine until now and here she was, sitting on a rock, licking a cornet and wanting him gone.

He hadn't come down to the beach to preach

the gospel according to him, as she'd described it. It was a matter of needing to know that she was all right, and maybe get some feedback on that kiss. But after the conversation they'd just had he was beginning to wonder if it had actually happened. If he'd made her even more disgruntled with him, it would be just another mountain to climb.

'Is Ronnie coming back, or what?' he asked.

'No. He would have done, but I told him not to, that I would stay until the light went and that would be it. After all, there are enough notices around the place to warn the people who come here of the currents and the fast tides.'

He was looking around him. The beach was deserted except for a man walking his dog, and the light was going already, so he said, 'The light has almost gone and I know the guy with the dog. He's one of my patients who has lived here all his life and isn't likely to get himself into any trouble down here with the comings and goings of the tides. So I'll walk you back to the village.'

'Do I have a choice?' she asked coolly, concealing her pleasure at the thought.

'No, you don't,' was the reply. 'I am not leaving you down here on your own. It will be dark soon and in future don't be so generous with your offers to our friendly neighbourhood lifeguard.'

'Don't be so crabby!' she exclaimed, unaware that he wasn't sure if his suggestion that she help out on the beach had been a good idea.

'I'm not,' he told her, 'but I know what you're like.'

'No, you don't!' she declared. 'I can be strong and inflexible if I have to…so take care.' She was smiling but it didn't reach her eyes and he wondered whether she was referring to the past or the present.

On the walk back to their respective dwellings they chatted about local events, the surgery, the weather, everything but themselves, and when they reached her gate she was wishing him goodnight and whizzing up the drive with her door key in hand as if she was wary of him asking to come in.

There had been no likelihood of that, he thought. The wish to do so had been there, but after the hurt he'd caused the other night it wouldn't be the right thing to do.

In the days that followed they both still kept to his suggestion that they cool it. Their only lapses had been *the* kiss and their meeting on the beach when she'd been filling in for Ronnie.

The only time they were in each other's company now was at the practice, and both kept contact there down to the minimum. She was miserable and lonely, and he was causing much speculation amongst his socialising friends by never being available when it was party time.

Harry was the only person who guessed what was going on and he said nothing but thought a lot, along the lines that Leo was crazy if he was keeping the young French doctor at a distance. She was good at the job, a charming young woman, and he was a great guy.

But remembering all the ups and downs and misunderstandings that he and Phoebe had had before it had all come right, he could sympathise with Leo, whose attractions seemed to cause more misery than pleasure in his life. But something told him that Amelie would not be swayed by outward appearances, she would need more than that.

The stalemate between them was still in place the week of the Big Summer Picnic that was held on the field behind the village hall. It was free, the only thing asked of those who attended was that they bring their own food and drinks, otherwise it wouldn't be a picnic.

Amelie was looking forward to it as something to break into the routine she had fallen into of surgery and beach on weekdays, and the beach again for most of the weekend.

One of the most painful things about cooling it with Leo was them living so close to each other. When she looked across at his apartment it was as if it was a tree bearing forbidden fruit, beckoning her to come and taste. She sighed at the stupidity of the way they were behaving, but if ever they were to put an end to the painful pretence they were involved in, Leo would have to be the one to do it because it had come from him.

He looked on the closeness of their homes as a mixed blessing. It was comforting to know she was so near, but agonising not to be able to talk to her, hold her, and the blame for that was his alone for not facing up to the past.

Until now he'd never met anyone who'd made him feel uneasy about the memory time warp he was caught up in, but with the coming of Amelie a voice in his mind was telling him to look to the future and forget the past. But he'd lived with the memory of Delphine for a long time, so would he be able to put it to one side and find happiness with Amelie?

Most of the surgery staff were going to the Big Summer picnic and, knowing how interested she was in any local event, he was pretty sure she would be amongst them. So if nothing else they would be around each other for a few hours if the warm lazy days of summer that had become a regular thing over the last few weeks didn't disappoint the picnickers.

He'd promised the vicar's wife he would be around all the time in case of accident or injury, and knew that Harry would also be there with Phoebe and little Marcus. And with Amelie also amongst those present, health and safety would be well represented should the need arise.

He had been right when he'd thought that Amelie wouldn't want to miss the picnic. The days were long without him in her life when she was away from the surgery. Even the time on the beach with Ronnie, which she really enjoyed, didn't make up for his absence. So *she* was hoping *he* would be at the picnic, if only for the chance to be near him in a less restricted way than when they were working.

She set off for the village hall with a picnic basket optimistically holding enough for two, and knew she could be asking for a disappointment, yet it was worth a try.

He was there before her, supervising the erection of a carousel beside the large marquee that was always provided in case of rain. But today the skies were blue and the sun was beaming down graciously on to the scene below.

There was excitement in the air and soon the community feeling that such occasions brought forth would take over with a local band in place and the revellers ready to enjoy themselves.

Leo had seen her arrive and his spirits lifted. So far so good, he thought. The moment he was free he was going to go over and ask if he might join her, and if Amelie said yes he would take it from there, and if she said no, well…

She was chatting to Ronnie and his family, who had just arrived, and the last thing he wanted was for her to be drawn into their circle.

Jenna and Lucas hadn't arrived yet and surprisingly neither had Harry and Phoebe, but no doubt they were on their way. Then all the folks he enjoyed being with would be there, with his lovely French doctor top of the list.

The hierarchy of the Balfour family were expected, but would not be staying long as it might get too noisy for Barbara in her frail state. But she was insisting on attending, as anything that gave her the opportunity to be with those who were looking after her beloved practice in the same way that she had was a pleasure that didn't come often enough.

As they'd been about to leave the headland to take the road into the village, she'd asked Keith to turn the wheelchair round so that she could see the scene that was as familiar as her own face.

The sea bounding onto the golden sand with the same kind of power and purpose that she'd once had, and the cliffs rising towards them, worn by the sea and kissed by the sun with seabirds swirling above them, and in the distance the green and fertile fields of Devonshire.

'I love this place more than life itself, Keith,' she'd told her husband.

'Yes, I know you do,' had been his gentle reply, and he'd pointed the wheelchair towards the village once more.

'When we get there, put me in a sheltered spot under a tree, will you?' she asked. 'I'm going to have a nap before everyone begins to arrive.'

'Yes, anything you say,' he told her, and thought he must have said that a thousand times in their long life together.

When they reached the main street there were lots of folk about and they waved or called across to them, and Keith thought Bluebell Cove was

Barbara's reason for living. It happened all the time when he took her out. The respect and affection that was always there went a long way to make up for her having to retire because of her lack of mobility, which had been followed by serious heart defects, but he knew more than anyone that inside she was the same old battling Barbara whose patients had been her life's blood.

There was only a scattering of folks there when they arrived at the field behind the village hall. Soon there would be lots of noise and excitement and then they would leave as it would be too much for his frail wife.

So he did as she'd asked, left her to rest in a secluded spot with the branches of an old oak tree protecting her from the rays of the sun, and went to have a word with Leo, who was helping members of the events committee erect the various kinds of amusements that would be there to entertain the picnickers.

There was no sign of Harry and Jenna, the other two Balfours, but both had young children to cope with and Keith and Leo were not unduly surprised. It would be unheard of for the members of that family not to be present on such an occasion.

As Amelie watched the two men chatting together, she had no idea that Keith had claimed Leo's attention just as he was about to approach her, so she was envisaging spending the time with Ronnie's family, who were lovely but not who she wanted to be with today.

Leaving her picnic basket on a nearby table, she began to stroll around the field, admiring the sideshows and carousel and taking note of the instruments, mainly guitars and drums, already in position on the stage.

As she came to the end of the field where there was less to see she gave a casual glance in the direction of the wheelchair and its occupant and paused. She'd only spoken to Barbara Balfour once, when she'd been invited to supper at Harry's, and had liked the elderly doctor's straightforward manner.

Feeling that she looked rather lonely there beneath the trees, Amelie went across to speak to her. As she approached it seemed that she was asleep with her head back and eyes closed, but when she reached her side she saw that it wasn't sleep that was holding her so still. She'd seen it so many times before in hospital.

By this time Keith had gone to talk to other friends and Leo, who had been observing Amelie's progress around the field, was about to join her. He could see her at the far end, bending over Barbara, and thought it was good that the two of them were getting to know each other.

When she looked around her to call for help he was coming towards her, and she cried, 'Leo! Come quickly!' then turned back to the woman in the wheelchair. He was by her side in seconds and saw to his dismay that she was trying to resuscitate Barbara who, at a glance, had already passed on to another life.

'It's no use. You are too late, Amelie,' he said sombrely. 'It could have happened some time before you found her and with no one around to see, she probably had a massive heart attack and was gone.'

So far they had been unobserved but now Keith was on his way back to check on his wife and something in the way they were bending over her made him quicken his step. When he stood looking down at the woman who had given her life to her patients and left only a little of it for her husband and child, he said soberly, 'I think she knew it wouldn't be long. As we were setting off to come here Barbara asked me to stop while she had what turned out to be a last look from the top of the headland at all the places she loved so much.'

'Jenna and Lucas have just arrived. Will one of you go and fetch her? It will be a great shock, though again maybe it won't. I feel that Lucas, as Barbara's cardiac consultant, will have prepared Jenna for this.'

'I'll go, Amelie, if you'll stay here with Keith,' Leo said, and she nodded gravely. Soon the field would be full of those out to enjoy the day. It was vital he get to Jenna quickly.

He found her chatting to friends with Lucas holding Lily in his arms, but his expression caused the chatter to dwindle into silence and into it he said gently, 'It's your mother, Jenna. Amelie found her a few moments ago down at the bottom of the field. She tried to resuscitate her but I'm afraid it was too late.'

Lucas passed the baby to one of their friends and with his arm around Jenna's shoulders they followed him to where Keith was seated by his wife's body on a chair that Amelie had found for him.

From that moment of extreme sadness the news began to filter around the field that battling Barbara Balfour had fought her last fight, that a failing heart had been the victor this time.

An announcement was made to say that Barbara had passed away and a minute's silence was called for before the local undertaker and his assistants arrived to take her to the chapel of rest.

There having been three doctors present, one of them her cardiac consultant who had seen her in the last few days, it meant there would be no necessity for an inquest, and everyone present stood with heads bowed as the sad little procession left the field.

When the vicar would have cancelled the event Keith had said not to, that, knowing Barbara's love of Bluebell Cove and its inhabitants, she would want it to proceed, and with that thought in mind the band began to play again, the carousel began to turn, and children ran around excitedly, exactly how Barbara would have wanted it to be.

When the picnic was over Amelie and Leo walked back towards the surgery together. The events of the afternoon had made their differences seem minor. They'd managed the time together that they'd been yearning for, but under the worst possible circumstances, and still there was no sign of Harry.

'Where can they be?' Leo said as they sat in the garden of the house.

'It will hit Harry hard, losing Barbara. From what he's told me, the Balfours were good to him when his parents lost his little brother and were so wrapped up in their grief that he got pushed to one side. It was Barbara who persuaded him to come back to Bluebell Cove when he lost his wife, and it was here that he met Phoebe, who he adores.'

At that moment Leo's mobile rang and when he picked it up Harry's voice came over the line. 'I thought I might find you at Amelie's place,' he said. 'I take it that the picnic is over.' His voice had a lift to it that had to mean he didn't know that Barbara was no longer in the background of his life as she had been for so long.

'Er…yes,' Leo said uncomfortably, dreading what was coming next,

But Harry forestalled him by announcing

jubilantly. 'We have a daughter, Leo! Phoebe and I have daughter and Marcus a little sister. Did you wonder where we were? She went into labour a couple of weeks early in the middle of the night, so we wrapped Marcus, who was sound asleep, in a blanket and drove to the maternity unit at Hunter's Hill. The baby arrived just before lunch.'

'That is wonderful news! Are they both all right?'

'They're fine and so is Marcus, who is trying to take it all in and wanting lots of love. I'm on top of the world, Leo, and must go as the obstetrician is due on his rounds any moment.'

'Before you go, there is something that you need to know,' Leo told him sombrely, wishing himself anywhere but at the other end of the line to the ecstatic new father. 'Your Aunt Barbara passed away at the picnic this afternoon. I am so sorry to be the bearer of such sad tidings in the midst of your joy, Harry.'

There was silence for a long moment then

Harry said chokingly, 'What time did she die, Leo?'

'The church clock had just struck one when Amelie found her under the trees in the wheel-chair. Why, what are you thinking?'

'That was the time our daughter came into the world. I had a feeling that it might be. As one life ended, another was beginning. Where are Keith and Jenna? I must speak to them.'

'They are all back at the house on the head-land. Hopefully your wonderful news will help to lessen their heartache a little.'

Leo's expression was sombre as he put the phone down and Amelie thought that Antoine had done her a favour when he'd turned his attention to another woman. If he hadn't, she would now be living a mundane life with a mun-dane husband. Would never have met the man sitting opposite her who had just done his best to soften the blow he'd inflicted on Harry in the midst of his rejoicing.

He was so special, she was so happy to be

with him, and if they were going to continue as they had been without any possibility of a future together, at least she would have had the joy of knowing him.

Yet as he sat there dejectedly, having just turned Harry's euphoria into grief, she couldn't sit and watch and do nothing. Going across to him, she placed her arm around his shoulders and said softly, 'Don't feel bad, Leo. You had to tell him before he heard it on the village grape-vine. Until now Keith and Jenna haven't known where he was to tell him about Barbara's pass-ing. Better that it came from you.'

He nodded then, getting slowly to his feet, said, 'You were wonderful out there, but what a shame it had to be you who found her. Though I suppose it was a blessing in one way. Keith and Jenna were spared the sharp, agonising shock that is part of a sudden death by having you and I around.

'We work well together, don't we? And today I was hoping we might have played together at the picnic, but the fates had other ideas. Playful was the last thing I felt after what happened to Barbara.'

'So why don't we go for a walk where it is calm and peaceful and we can unwind? Then find a nice restaurant for dinner, my treat,' she suggested. 'There is nothing more we can do here.'

CHAPTER SEVEN

TO AVOID going anywhere near the headland and the Balfours' house, which was now in mourning, Amelie and Leo walked inland between hedgerows weighed down with flowers, and past Wheatlands, the biggest farm in the area, owned by the well-respected Enderby family.

While Amelie was observing its opulence, he said, 'Some spread, isn't it? Would you like to live in a place like that?'

She considered for a moment and then said, 'No. I don't think so. I'm not keen on large houses.'

'You mean like your family's chateau?'

She smiled across at him. 'You have it in one. My parents took it for granted that I wanted to be married in the chateau when I was engaged to Antoine. In fact, that's where the wedding was to be held.'

'But you didn't want to?'

'No. And now I will never be married in that place. If I ever got close to marriage again, which I seriously doubt I will, I would choose to have my wedding somewhere small and beautiful.'

'Like you,' he said in a low voice, and she turned away.

'Don't make fun of me,' she told him. 'You're the one with the looks.'

'And do you think I care about that?' he exclaimed. 'I'd rather be downright ugly than the village catch.'

She was laughing now and he thought how easy she was to be with. How uncomplicated her attitude to life was, or had been until he'd begun to cause confusion in her mind.

She was happy to be with him if he would let her, like now, but knew that could change if his conscience began to pull at the strings of his integrity again.

'So where are we going to eat?' he asked as a restaurant with a thatched roof appeared on the skyline. 'The place ahead is very popular. It is where Lucas proposed to Jenna over a clotted-cream tea on a cold day when the place was empty, or so she thought. Her family and friends were hiding in one of the other rooms ready to congratulate them when she'd said yes.'

'How lovely, but supposing she'd said no?'

'I take it you've seen Lucas Devereux?'

'Well, yes, of course.'

'There you have your answer, then, and in case you're thinking that it wasn't very romantic, being proposed to while eating a scone covered with jam and cream, surely we both agree that it is the people involved that matter rather than the location.'

'Quite,' she agreed demurely, 'as long as it isn't in the fish sheds down by the harbour, or on top of the refuse collection pile.'

If she'd been less confused about his feelings, she might have rounded off the comment with *so*

do please bear that in mind, but there was nothing in his manner to indicate that he'd changed
his mind about what he'd said when he'd spelt
out for her that they weren't going anywhere
together on a permanent basis.

The restaurant wasn't as near as it had looked.
When they were almost halfway there Leo said,
'I know a short cut. No use when in a car but
much quicker when on foot. It is through remote
woodland for part of the way but will certainly
get us there more quickly. Do you want to try
it?'

'Yes,' she agreed. 'I don't know about you but
I'm hungry.' *And not just for food, she would
have liked to have told him.*

The woods felt cool after being in the evening
sun and everywhere was very still. After a while
Leo said, 'Shall we rest for a few moments, if
you can get your hunger pangs to subside?'

'Yes. I think I can,' she replied. 'Appetite will
have to take second place to feet. We passed

a stream only moments ago. I'm going to cool them off in it. Are you coming?'

'No, I'm fine here. Don't be too long or the place we're heading for will be full.'

She was already removing the sandals she was wearing and walking carefully towards the edge of a narrow rivulet running through the woods.

While she was gone he took a large clean handkerchief out of his pocket and when she came back and lay down on the grass beside him he began to dry her feet with gentle strokes.

She ached for him, Amelie thought as he bent to his task, but of his own free will Leo had taken desire out of their relationship because of something she still didn't fully understand, so maybe it was up to her to bring it back.

He looked up and found her bright blue gaze on him. 'What?' he questioned. 'What are you thinking?'

'I'm thinking that not so long ago I accused you of having never kissed me or made love to me, didn't I?'

His voice was flat. 'Yes, you did indeed.'

'So you dealt with one of the omissions that day in the lay-by, but so far haven't done anything about the other.'

'And you would like me to do so, is that it?'

'Only if you want to, but I must warn you I am no expert. It will be a first time.'

Was she serious? he thought raggedly. Amelie had no idea of the workings of his mind when it came to his personal life or she wouldn't have created this sort of situation.

It was another opportunity to tell her about Delphine, but to her it might come over as just another rejection, an escape route back to his life before she'd come on the scene.

The eyes looking up into his were wide and questioning. 'You don't want me, do you?' she cried, humiliated beyond reason. 'Why does my mouth always have to be ahead of my mind when I'm with you?'

He had no answer to that. Instead he said in

the same flat tone, 'I think we should be on our way if you are as hungry as you said.'

'I've just lost my appetite,' she told him. 'Food would choke me.'

'You might change your mind when we get there,' he said placatingly. 'So up you get and off we go in search of it. Just one thing before we go, Amelie. You have just put yourself amongst almost every woman I meet. They all want me to bed them.'

'And do you?'

'You mean am I the local stud? I can't believe you're asking me that. I thought you were different, but it seems I was wrong.'

She was up and running, wanting to get as far away from him as possible so that he wouldn't realise just how much he'd humiliated her. But he was moving fast behind her and when he caught up said, 'Watch out for tree roots, Amelie,' as if they'd never had that dreadful conversation.

For the rest of the evening they were so polite to each other it was nauseating. But all the time the thought was rocketing around her mind that once again she had been the unwanted. And, she thought shamefully, she'd even mentioned her virginity like some sort of special offer.

She couldn't wait to get away from him so that her shame might be a more private thing. The moment they'd finished eating she went to pay for the meal, in keeping with her promise when she'd suggested they go for a walk and she could tell from his expression that he wasn't pleased about that either.

'I've asked them to order us a taxi,' he said when she returned to the table. 'I didn't think you would want to walk back the way we came.'

'How right you are,' she said quietly. 'I never ever want to set foot in those woods again.'

'I meant no hurt by what I said,' he told her. 'You are young, vulnerable and enchanting. Can we just leave it at that and be friends?'

'If you say so,' she said bleakly, not to be comforted or given back her self-respect. At that moment they were told that their taxi was outside and she hurried towards the means of escape from her folly.

When it pulled up outside the house she didn't give Leo the chance to make any further comments, she had its door open and was running up the drive with door key at the ready once again. By the time he'd paid the driver she had disappeared from sight and he thought grimly the chances of her opening the door again if he rang the bell were slim.

So he made his way to his apartment and spent the next hour going over the awful events of the day that had started with discovering that Barbara Balfour was no longer with them, and ended with his refusal to do something he'd been aching to do for weeks—make love to Amelie.

The incident had been catastrophic in many ways. She'd taken him by surprise, for one thing, and another reason of a more irksome kind had been that it had been she who had done the asking.

It was clear that she hadn't been remembering his words of wisdom with regard to cooling their relationship at that moment. So where on earth did they go from here? Was he still so tied to the heartache of the past that he couldn't make love to Amelie when the opportunity was there?

He'd felt as if she was expecting him to jump at the chance when she'd made the request and had seen red. Of course he'd wanted to, but not under those circumstances.

When the phone rang he was praying that it might be her, but it was Jenna on the line with details of her mother's funeral and also with the news that Ethan was coming over from France for it on his own as both Ben and Kirstie were now at school there and after the upheaval of the move he and Francine didn't want to have to disrupt their education again.

'How is your father taking it?' he asked. and was surprised by her reply.

'Very well, considering. He has amazed us all by saying that now Mum has gone he's going to sell the house and travel the world, something he has always wanted to do but never got the chance. So what do you think of that?'

'Good luck to him. Do you think he will have any trouble selling Four Winds?'

'He might. The market is unpredictable at the moment.'

'If he goes ahead with his plans, I can find him a buyer.'

'Really! Who?'

'Me.'

'He would be happy about that, Leo. You and Amelie were so kind to him when Mum died, and he has always liked you. If he does keep to what he is saying you will be the first to know, and now I must go as Lily is fretful tonight, almost as if she knows that her grandma isn't here any more.'

As he rang off he couldn't believe that he'd just said he would like to buy her parents' house if it came up for sale, and more unbelievable still that he'd had Amelie's love of Bluebell Cove in mind when he'd said it.

The apartment was good enough for him on his own, but it was not the sort of place he would want to bring his bride to if the church bells ever pealed out over the village for him. Acquiring the house might be easy enough, but as for the rest of it he was losing his sense of direction.

In the house across the way Amelie was weeping tears of humiliation and regret. She'd known it had been a big mistake to say what she had to Leo the moment the words had come out of her mouth.

While he'd been drying her feet, desire had risen in her in a hot tide. She'd craved his touch like a thirsty person for water, with disastrous results, and as if asking him to make love to her hadn't been awful enough, she'd told him about the icing on the cake!

The right thing to do would be to go back to France, she kept telling herself, but she was committed to working at the practice for six months and didn't want to break her contract. There was some time to go before it would be up, so all she could do was to continue avoiding Leo as much as possible.

It was the picnic and what had happened to Barbara Balfour that had thrown them so much into each other's company again, and those moments in the tranquil woodland setting had tempted her to say what was in her heart, but the vast waters of the sea would freeze over before she ever did that again.

She was halfway up the stairs on her way to bed when she caught sight of Leo through the landing window, striding across from the apartment, and quickly shrank back out of sight.

The day was almost over. It had been a ghastly one, and much as the sight of him always warmed her heart, enough was enough. She was too spent for any further conversation between them and what he could possibly want of her after the way they'd separated when the taxi had dropped them off she really didn't know.

Yet one thing she could be sure of—he wasn't coming across because he was having second thoughts about his refusal to do what she'd asked.

She was right on that count. Leo was coming to tell her about Jenna's phone call. To inform her that Barbara's funeral was to take place on the coming Friday and that if they could both be spared from the practice, he felt they owed it to Keith to be there, having been with him when he'd discovered that his wife had died.

But there was no answer when he rang the bell and when he looked up, the curtains had been drawn in the master bedroom. So the excuse he'd been going to use to see Amelie for just one more time before the day was done was not going to work. With measured steps he returned to his apartment.

She had heard him ring the bell from up above

and was lying with her head beneath the pillows to shut out its noise. When it stopped she pulled the covers up around her and, too exhausted to even think any more, turned on her side and slept.

She awoke to a room full of sunlight and the sound of the church bells pealing not far away, and thought thankfully that it was Sunday. She had twenty-four hours to gather her wits before she and Leo came face to face again.

It was not to be the case. He came as she was finishing a mundane breakfast of cereal, toast and tea. This time she had to let him in. He'd seen her seated at the dining table as he'd walked up the drive and his first words when she opened the door to him were, 'Are you all right after yesterday?'

'Yes, I suppose so,' she told him, and before he had the chance to say anything else she added, 'Have you heard when the funeral is?'

'Yes, Jenna phoned late last night. I came

across to tell you but there was no answer so I presumed you had gone to bed. It is on Friday at half past two for a private family service at the crematorium, followed by a public thanksgiving service in the church for Barbara's life and her dedication to those she served so well in a medical capacity. I spoke to Harry a few moments ago and he said the church service is to be relayed to anyone who can't get inside, indicating that a large attendance is expected.

'They're talking of changing the name of the surgery to the Balfour Medical Centre, which I feel would be very fitting, don't you? Especially as with Harry in charge there is still a Balfour involved.'

'Er, yes,' she agreed, taking in the image of him, drawn looking around the eyes but dressed in a smart top and jeans as if the events of the previous day had never taken place, while she was huddled at the table in an old T-shirt and shorts. But maybe that was because she cared and he didn't.

Yet she knew that wasn't true. He did care, but not in the way that she cared for him. She adored him. The more she saw of him the more she wanted to be near him, but yesterday had shown that they weren't going anywhere together.

He had a surprise for her and it brought her out of the doldrums into amazement. 'The family want you to read the lesson at the service in the church, if you will.'

'I don't know!' she gasped. 'I am a stranger here. What will those who have known Dr Balfour all their lives think of that? And though I speak English fluently, I do not always get it right.'

'You will,' he said confidently, 'and I won't be far away.'

As if, she thought. He might be near in body, but in mind and purpose he might as well be sitting on the moon instead of in a nearby pew. Yet she couldn't refuse, not about something like that, so she told him weakly. 'Tell them yes, I will do as they ask. But I hope that it will not offend.'

'It won't,' he assured her. 'Everyone knows that you found her and tried to save her, and now I must go. An acquaintance of mine, Georgina, who owns the boutique next to the post office, was taken ill with some kind of gastritis during the night and phoned to ask me to go round, and as she lives alone I stayed with her.'

'I see.'

'Yes, I'm sure you do,' he said dryly. 'The farmer who delivers the milk around here gave me a wink when he saw me coming out of there at six o'clock this morning. I'm going home to get some sleep now, Amelie, and am presuming that you are going to spend the day on the beach, helping Ronnie.'

'Yes, that is my intention when I have gathered my wits together,' she said stiffly, and with a sudden surge of jealousy said, 'Does your friend at the boutique not know that you are off duty at the weekend, that she should have called an emergency doctor?'

'I would expect she does,' he said, 'but what are friends for, Amelie?'

He was already moving towards the door and as if he hadn't made her miserable enough the day before, he departed with a wave of the hand and the casual observation that he would see her around, no doubt.

Of course he would *see her around*, she thought glumly when he'd gone. They both worked at the practice, didn't they? She would have that small comfort, if nothing else.

When she arrived there on the Monday morning it was as if a cloud of sadness was hanging over the place because the woman who had served it so well for many years until her own health had brought her to a halt had succumbed to a massive heart attack.

Lucy, who liked to chat before the day began, was white faced and silent. She had been Barbara

Balfour's one and only close friend, had known her faults and her failings just as well as she'd known the woman's dedication to her calling.

They'd called her 'battling Barbara' but Lucy knew that her battles had never been for herself. They'd been with the authorities when she'd thought they had been failing a patient, or with the hospital if she'd thought they had been dragging their feet regarding appointments.

If Lucy had been close to her, so had Harry, especially during his young years. Phoebe had asked him if he would like their new baby daughter to be christened Barbara, but always one to call a spade a spade he'd said with a wry smile, 'It's a lovely thought, Phoebe, but I don't want our innocent little one to be called after my aunt, even though I had the greatest respect for her.

'She was a fantastic doctor, served her patients to the limit of her endurance, but when it came to her family, she fell far short. We both know loving families are what it's all about, and while we're on the subject I do not want to call our baby after Cassie either, as you once suggested.'

'My life with her wasn't a bed of roses by any means, so no to Cassie. The only name that warms my heart is yours, and if we can find one just as beautiful, that will be it.'

Amelie had been treating Leo with cool politeness since arriving at the surgery and every time anyone mentioned the funeral looming up on Friday she wished herself miles away because he had said he would be there for her and she didn't want him to feel it was something else she required of him on sufferance.

In the meantime, the waiting room was filling up with those who had problems of their own to contend with and would be expecting her to pull a cure out of the hat, or at the least some relief from the ills of body and mind.

Her first patient of the day was Martha Maguire, cook at the village school. She had itchy weals all over her skin, with yellowish white centres surrounded by inflammation.

When asked the usual questions regarding eating different foods not usually part of her diet, changing to a different kind of washing powder or the possibility of garden hazards, there didn't seem to be any answers to explain the rash.

'It looks like urticaria,' Amelie told her, 'or nettle rash, as it is sometimes known, and is rarely serious, except in cases when other illnesses are present, such as lupus erythematosus or vaculitis. It usually clears up without too much fuss by using calamine lotion for the raised areas on the skin and antihistamine tablets for inward treatment of the irritation. I'll give you supplies of both. Come back if there is no improvement during the next few days.'

Martha was smiling. 'Thanks, Doctor. Sounds like I made a fuss about nothing, but working in a school one is open to all the children's illnesses. Some of the parents send them when they should be at home, and even though what I've got isn't serious, I'm going to have to stay at home as they won't want me to handle food with a rash, and I don't blame them.'

'You didn't fuss over nothing, Mrs Maguire. It is always best to be sure when something strange happens to our bodies,' she told her.

Jonah Trelfa, who'd been a patient with a heart problem on her first day at the practice, followed the school cook. He'd come for a repeat prescription of the medication the hospital had put him on that day and was looking much fitter than he had done then.

As he lowered himself on to the seat opposite he said, 'I've just seen Dr Fenchurch going into the boutique. Is Georgina poorly?'

'I'm afraid I have no idea, Mr Trelfa,' she told him politely, acutely aware that Leo was giving his friend his full attention in whatever way she was demanding it. Yet she had to have a rethink when an ambulance came screeching along the road and stopped outside the shop. Seconds later paramedics came out with its owner on a stretcher and Leo by her side.

He watched as it disappeared from sight, then turned and went back into the shop. He was at the surgery when the staff stopped for lunch, and when about to go to the baker's across the way asked if he could bring her anything.

Her reply was 'No, thank you.' And before she could ask about his friend, he nodded as if her refusal wasn't unexpected and went on his way.

By the time he came back there was no need to ask about the boutique owner. The news was filtering around the surgery that she had been taken into hospital with gastroenteritis.

She'd just said 'I see' when he'd told her he'd been in the boutique most of the night. But it must have been the way she'd said it that had prompted him to tell her about the milk delivering farmer's reaction when he'd seen him coming out of there.

She wanted to tell him she was sorry, yet what had she done wrong?

When he'd told her where he'd been during

the night, she'd been too overwrought about the episode in the woods to take too much notice, and in any case did it matter?

He kept making it clear that he didn't want her, so why should he be blamed if he had a yearning for someone else, and in any case it hadn't been like that, he'd gone to answer a cry for help in his capacity as a doctor.

At the end of the day he caught her up as she was leaving and said casually, 'Is it the beach again tonight?'

'Er, yes,' she replied, and before he could say anything else went on, 'Have you heard how your friend is?'

'Yes. She's quite poorly. Last night it was severe stomach pains. I felt that she might have some degree of food poisoning that would clear itself, as it often does, but it was much worse this morning so I had her admitted to hospital.

'Georgina's mother is on her way from the Scilly Isles to be with her while she gets over this, so it should all end happily enough once she is clear of the infection, which is not always the case, is it, Amelie?'

She was her usual direct self as she asked, 'Are you referring to us?'

'I might be.'

'What happened on Saturday was my fault, Leo. It was stupid of me. Over the years I've learned never to take anything for granted. It helped a lot when Antoine dumped me for the red-haired nurse, but I didn't bring caution into play when I let my feelings get the better of me while you were drying my feet. So will you accept my apology?'

He groaned softly. 'You have nothing to be sorry about, Amelie. I also let my feelings get the better of me, so we're quits.'

'I thought we were on the same wavelength until yesterday,' she told him, 'even though you do have reservations, but it seems as if I was way out.'

They were at her gate. She was ready to do her quick skip up the drive, but he wasn't going to let her do it this time, at least not until he'd said his piece.

Gripping her arm, he swung her round to face him and said tightly, 'Do you want it on the drive, in the sitting room, the bath, or more traditionally on the bed?'

'What are you talking about?' she cried.

'Making love, of course. Surely I don't have to spell it out.'

The heat of anger was replacing the chill of the question she'd just asked. 'Oh, yes, you do! Thanks for offering to oblige me, but, *no, thanks.*'

She wrenched herself out of his grip and he made no move to stop her. Turning, he walked slowly towards the apartment, unlocked the door at the bottom of the wooden staircase and proceeded upwards, considering as he did so what he would have done if she'd taken him at his word.

When he'd gone Amelie shut the door behind her and stood in the hallway with cheeks flaming and eyes sparking fire as it registered that Leo had been telling her in a roundabout sort of way that he would do the asking if there was any to be done. Well, so much for that. He could ask until he was blue in the face from now on.

Barbara Balfour took her last ride through Bluebell Cove in a glass-sided coach on four wheels pulled by black horses that tossed the plumes on their heads proudly as they passed the silent crowds lining the pavements.

They were on the way to the private family service and Amelie, sitting next to Leo in one of the funeral cars, had a feeling that they were going to be paired off during both of the services that had been arranged.

Every woman's dream man and the nondescript French doctor as a twosome were bound to result in raised eyebrows in some quarters.

CHAPTER EIGHT

AMELIE'S surmise that she would be partnered with Leo had been correct and it had been a relief when the funeral was over and they had returned to the practice where a reduced staff had kept the place going during the absence of the three doctors and Lucy.

To Leo's amazement, Keith Balfour had taken him to one side after the service in the church and asked if he'd meant what he'd said to Jenna about buying his house.

He'd been the patient and loving husband of a difficult woman for many years and was now a changed character, already making plans for a world cruise with the intention of coming back from it to a newly built apartment on the coast road.

'Yes, I was serious,' Leo had told him. 'Four Winds is in a fantastic position. Whenever you feel ready, I will be only too pleased to discuss buying it. There is no rush,' he'd assured the older man with a dismal reminder of Amelie's closed countenance during the two services.

The only time it had lightened had been when she'd stood in front of the mourners in the old Norman church and reverently done what had been asked of her by the Balfour family, reciting in her precise English the reading they had chosen.

He'd been near while she'd done it, as he'd promised he would be, but he might as well have been invisible for all the notice she'd taken of him, and if he hadn't been so keen to buy Four Winds House he might have been less enthusiastic when its owner had brought up the subject.

'I'm off on my world cruise in a few weeks,' Keith had told him in reply to him saying there was no rush, 'and would like it to be settled before I go, if that's all right with you.'

He'd assured him that it would be, even though his original interest had not been from the point of view of living there alone.

Autumn was on the brink, he'd thought as he'd returned to the surgery after the funeral. Days were shortening, harvests were being brought in, and even with a ready-made buyer for his property Keith Balfour wasn't going to have contracts signed before he went, but surely they could trust each other?

Amelie was back before him and already seeing a patient, but Harry had gone back to the hospital with Marcus to be with Phoebe and the baby, so there would be his patients to add to their lists today and some catching up to do as well.

When surgery was over at last, he put aside his longing to be with Amelie and drove to the hospital to bring Georgina and her mother home. The boutique owner was due to be discharged in the early evening and that would be one less worry on his mind.

She was just a friend who would have liked to have been more, but he'd made it clear that his feelings didn't match hers. His concern over her had been just that of an acquaintance, the kind of thing he would do for anyone in distress, and now that her mother had arrived he could step back and let her take over.

Amelie watched him drive off and felt the melancholy of the day increase.

Leo hadn't spoken to her since the funeral. Keith had buttonholed him and by the time he'd been free she'd been back at the surgery, trying to catch up from her absence earlier.

It would seem that he'd gone to visit Georgina, she thought miserably. She understood the other woman's need of his presence, yet he could have said something, if only goodbye, before he'd gone.

Maybe he felt he'd seen enough of her for one day, and on that thought she went back to the house, had a quick bite, and went down to the beach to keep the amiable Ronnie company.

Storm clouds were gathering when she got there and those present were hurriedly packing up their belongings and getting ready for the off before there was a deluge. Ronnie followed them soon after, not expecting to be needed after the general exodus, and Amelie was about to do the same when she was halted in her tracks by the appearance of an anxious mother who announced that they couldn't find their youngest child, a four-year-old boy called Freddie.

'I thought he was with his dad up in the front of the bus and he thought he was with me at the back with our twin girls,' she said frantically, 'and we can't find him. He is a little wanderer if he gets the chance.' She looked around her anxiously. 'The tide is going out, isn't it?'

She didn't get a reply. Amelie had gone round a bend on the rocky part of the shore to see if the child was playing in the next inlet, but the strip of sand was bare of anyone, especially a small child. Yet as she scanned the foam-tipped waves that were surging back to where they'd come from she saw a small blond head above them, rising and falling with each movement of the sea as it departed.

She called to the child's mother just once, then flung herself into the water and was immediately aware of the pull of the current beneath her. It was then that her swimming prowess came to her aid. Gathering up all her strength, she grabbed the little boy and began to fight her way back to shore, but with every stroke she slid further out and the child she was holding began to struggle and scream.

When a head of damp golden fairness bobbed up beside her she was overwhelmed with relief, and when the voice she'd been longing to hear bellowed above the crashing waves, 'Let him go, Amelie. I've got him,' together they fought their way back to the shore with Leo holding the protesting child.

'Where is Ronnie?' Leo spluttered angrily as he bent over the child, who was lying limply on the wet sand and whimpering softly. 'You could both have been drowned. The currents out there had a mind of their own tonight. He needs to be checked over in A and E and neither of us have a phone handy. Where are his parents?'

'Here they are,' she said as Freddie's frantic parents came running across the sand. 'His mother came back down here after they'd left to avoid the rain that was threatening because they couldn't find him and had left his father searching for him at the top.'

She observed Freddie, who was now sitting up. 'Shall we give them back their precious little one?'

A crowd had been watching their endeavours from the cliffs and Freddie's parents, with arms outstretched and cries of relief and gratitude, were running towards them to claim their child.

'Have either of you got a mobile with you?' Leo asked as Freddie's mother wrapped him in a dry towel and hugged him to her, and his father turned anxiously to make sure their daughters were where he could see them.

'Yes, I have,' he said.

'Then may I?' Leo asked. 'I'm going to ring for an ambulance to take your child to A and E to be checked over. Fortunately his head was above the water most of the time so we can hope that he hasn't swallowed too much salty seawater, but he hasn't spoken since we rescued him so there could be some extent of trauma, and bruising where we had to hold him so tightly.'

'What brought you to the beach?' Amelie asked when there was just the two of them left beneath a golden harvest moon that had replaced the storm clouds.

'You, of course, I've just brought Georgina and her mother home from the hospital and wanted to tell you how beautifully you read the lesson this afternoon.'

'Why didn't you tell me then?' she enquired perversely.

'With the temperature at zero, I think not.'

She was shivering now in her wet bathing suit and he said quickly, 'Why don't we go back to either your place or mine and have a shower, followed by a glass of wine to celebrate bringing young Freddie safely on to dry land?'

There was no immediate reply to the suggestion. Amelie was imagining what she looked like and deciding it would take more than a shower and a glass of wine to rectify her appearance after her recent battle against the currents, yet what did it matter? There'd already been one demise in Bluebell Cove in recent days. Thank goodness they'd prevented another and a child's at that.

'Yes, all right,' she agreed, and went on to say, 'Better if we go to the house. There is a shower in the main bathroom and another in the master bedroom.'

'Fine,' he said easily, 'and how about when we've cleaned ourselves up I go for fish and chips?'

'Mmm, that would be nice,' she agreed weakly.

When she'd showered and shampooed the salt out of her hair Amelie put on a cotton robe with a tie belt and after fastening it at the waist got a man's equivalent out of the wardrobe, which Ethan had left behind. Knocking on the bathroom door, she called to Leo that she would leave it outside on the landing for him.

'It's all right, I'm decent. You can bring it in,' he replied, and she pushed the door back slowly to reveal him standing barefoot wrapped in a towel. He was a sight to see, six feet, trimly built, with broad shoulders rising above the towel and a scattering of golden hair across his chest.

They stood facing each other without speaking for what seemed an eternity then he took a step forward and loosened the ties around her waist, and with the release of them the smooth, perfect, lines of her nakedness were revealed. His glance went over them and he let the towel that was covering him fall to the floor.

The heat of the attraction they had for each other was like a bright flame engulfing them, willing them to let it consume them. He felt ready to put down the burden of grief that he had carried for so long, and be the person he'd once been. He had the beautiful woman in his arms to thank for that and as he bent his head to kiss the cleft between her breasts she stroked his hair gently. She was melting with the desire he was arousing in her and when he lifted his head and their glances held, he said softly, 'Maybe this will make up for what didn't happen in the woods.'

He felt her stiffen and knew he'd said the wrong thing, brought back the memory of her humiliation, and even before she spoke he knew what she was going to say.

'Nothing could make up for that, Leo, unless you can tell me why you pick me up then put me down all the time. It does nothing for my self-confidence.'

She was retying the belt on her robe to let him see that the moment was over, but he didn't need telling. For the first time he'd felt he could make love to her without Delphine's face before him and go on from there, but Amelie, unaware of his past heartache, had brought up the subject of some of her own.

He'd got the message and it was hurting like a knife thrust that he of all people, who was generally thought to be every woman's dream man, should be spurned by the only one he'd ever wanted.

Where had it all gone wrong? he thought bleakly as he told her, 'I'm going back to my place in the robe you've found for me and will take my wet clothes with me. I'll return it in the morning.'

He went swiftly down the stairs and out into the night. Seconds later she saw the door close behind him as he disappeared into his apartment, and she thought that the day had ended as it had begun: miserable, sad...and hurtful.

Slumped in a chair by the window, Leo gazed out into the darkness and wondered where the delight of them getting to know each other had disappeared to. It was ironic that Amelie, who he ached for so much, should turn away from him when so many others would have jumped at the chance.

He'd felt their relationship was back on course as they'd walked home from the beach but had been wrong. He was attracted to her because she was different from any woman he'd ever met. When he'd let the towel fall he'd known she wanted him as much as he wanted her, but the barrier he'd put up that night in the woods was still there.

Amelie hadn't made love with the Antoine guy or she wouldn't still be a virgin, and as the memory came back of her telling him that she wasn't very experienced in the art of love-making, tenderness washed over him at the thought of how she'd wanted him to be the first.

So what had he done? Torn a strip off her for being so honest and without guile, and ever since they'd seemed to be on a downward path.

On Monday morning the surgery was fully staffed and back to normal after Friday's funeral. Harry announced on his arrival that they had chosen the lovely name of Freya for their baby daughter and that her christening was to take place on the following Sunday.

When he and Leo were briefly closeted together before the day commenced he said, 'Jenna is going to be one of her godmothers and we would like you to be her godfather, if you will, Leo.'

He had noticed that his friend and partner in the practice was not his usual brisk and capable self, and that the young French doctor on loan to them wasn't exactly chirpy either, so it didn't need a lot of brain power to work out that the oddly matched pair were not as happy as of late. But Leo's pleasure at being asked to be a godparent at the christening brought a smile and a ready acceptance.

'All the staff will be at the christening,' Harry told him meaningfully, and this time Leo's smile was wry.

'Is that so?' was the reply.

There was a knock on the door and when Harry called out for whoever it was to come in, Amelie appeared, seeking their advice with regard to a patient with an illness she hadn't come across before.

Leaving her in the company of the head of the practice, Leo left the room with a brief 'good morning' to the woman of his dreams, who was observing him warily.

As he proceeded to his own consulting room he was thinking that it was going to be his turn to be taking part in something special on the coming Sunday. He had been there for Amelie when she'd read the lesson at the funeral service to celebrate the ending of a life, and now it was his turn to take part in a joyful ceremony to acknowledge the beginning of a life.

It would be a cause for rejoicing rather than grief, the christening of little Freya. Would Amelie be there for him, as he'd been there for her? He doubted it. Togetherness was beginning to seem like a thing of the past.

As his first patient of the day ambled in, Leo put his own affairs on hold and had a smile of welcome for the local barber, Ambrose Whittaker, who was a genial old tease, always wanting to know why Leo wouldn't let him give him a short back and sides.

But not today. His face was pale and puckered with pain as he lowered himself down onto the nearest chair. 'I was out in the *Molly Maid* yesterday and slipped on the deck,' he said as Leo observed him questioningly. 'I've hurt my back something awful and I can't feel my legs properly.

Ambrose's life revolved around two things— his barber's shop on the harbour front and his boat, *Molly Maid*. But today the only woman in his life was out of favour because he'd hurt himself on her timbers.

'Can you ease your shirt off and show me where the pain is?' Leo said.

'It's at the bottom of my back and down my legs,' he was told.

He examined the hardy old fellow carefully and pronounced, 'It could be pressure on a nerve root from the fall that is causing so much pain, but only the hospital can sort that out for you, Ambrose. If there is a prolapsed disc or pressure on a nerve, CT scanning or an MRI should reveal the cause.'

'I'm going to send for an ambulance to take you straight from here to A and E. Is there anyone I can get in touch with to go with you?'

He shook his grizzled head. 'Not unless the guy at the fishing-tackle shop next door could come with me, but he's only just finished looking after that young nephew of his who was hurt when his father crashed the car, and he has a business to run, don't forget. No. I'll be fine on my own just as long as they can sort out the pain.'

'I will prescribe you some painkillers,' Leo told him, 'and will ask someone from the chemist across the way to pop over with them while we're waiting for the ambulance. You should find movement easier once the pain is under control, but finding the source of it is vital to avoid permanent damage to your back.

'Take a seat in the waiting room, Ambrose, and once the ambulance arrives, the paramedics will help you carefully on board.' Knowing how much the boat meant to him, he asked, 'Where is the *Molly Maid*? Safe in the harbour, I hope.'

'Aye, that she is. No back pain on earth would stop me from seeing her safely anchored.'

It was lunchtime, and during the short break there was reference amongst the staff to the coming christening, but not from Amelie's direction. She didn't join in the conversation and Leo decided it meant she wasn't intending to go. If that was the case, it showed even more clearly that togetherness was not the order of the day... or the night!

For the moment he was prepared to let it ride. It was only Monday. There was the rest of the week to come before Sunday was upon them.

His main concern at the moment was that she might decide to pack her bags and go back to where she'd come from, which was unthinkable.

Amelie was delighted for Leo's sake that he was to be one of the godparents for Harry and Phoebe's baby. She knew he would fulfil the pledges he made at the christening to their fullest degree, and wondered why she could be so sure of his feelings about something like that yet be totally confused about the way he felt about her.

The other night it would have been wonderful to have given in to the longing that he aroused in her and she in him, but what he'd said had brought those awful moments in the woods back and taken all the magic from the moment.

Unaware that he'd been ready to put his memories of what had happened to Delphine behind him, Amelie was constantly wondering if she would be faced with his changing moods all the time if she gave herself up to him. She'd told him once how much she needed security and there would be no secure feeling to be got from that.

But one thing *was* clear. She wanted to be at the christening for him, as he'd been at the funeral for her, and tried to imagine what it would be like if it was their child being christened, a beautiful girl or boy with their father's golden fairness.

But that sort of thing was disappearing into the realms of fantasy. At present they were further away from that kind of magic than they'd ever been. So it was a matter of going to the christening as just a friend and keeping a low profile.

In the middle of a week made up of endless days and miserable nights there was a surprise in store for Amelie in the form of a phone call from her parents to say they were on two months' leave and were staying in a rented apartment in London until it was up.

'So when are you coming to see us?' her mother wanted to know.

'I'm not sure,' she told her as the shock of hearing her voice was beginning to subside. 'I'm working in general practice in a beautiful village in Devon, so it will have to be when I have some free time. I don't want to cause the two doctors I'm working with any inconvenience.'

'Fair enough,' was the reply, without any overtones of disappointment, and that had been it, but Lisette Benoir had sighed deeply as she'd replaced the phone. It was her husband's fault that she saw so little of her daughter and she was caught in the middle.

Their appearance in her life again had made Amelie feel threatened, though she didn't know why, and on one of the rare occasions when she and Leo spoke at the surgery he observed her keenly and asked, 'What's wrong?'

The temptation to tell him that he knew very well what was wrong was there, but she knew he was referring to her uneasy expression of that moment and told him stiffly, 'My parents are on vacation in London for the next two months. I've had a phone call out of the blue.'

'Really!' he exclaimed. 'And how do you feel about that?'

'That it was a duty call. I presume they got my number here from Ethan. The French hospital where I was based knew I had come to England at Ethan's suggestion.

'He didn't say anything about them trying to get in touch with me when he came over for the funeral, so it must have been only in the last couple of days they've tried to find me.'

'So what next? Are you going to go to see them?'

'Yes, when I can. I've told them my responsibilities are here in Bluebell Cove first and foremost.'

'I'll bet that went down like a lead balloon. How long is it since they last saw you?'

'A year. I will go one weekend, maybe on a Saturday for the day.'

'I'll take you there, if you like.'

Amelie could feel her colour rising. What was that supposed to mean? Was it a peace offering? The kind of thing he would do for anyone? Or a casual sort of reprimand aimed at her reluctance to make the effort? Or was Leo curious about the two high flyers who put lifestyle before caring?

He hadn't mentioned his family much, but he'd said once how it had been stressful when he'd first joined the practice, travelling backwards and forwards to Manchester to look after his mother who had suddenly become quite ill with a chest and breathing problem.

So there had been no reluctance to put family first on his part, and if the practice had been in the charge of anyone other than Ethan at that time, he might have had to quit living and working in one of England's most beautiful counties.

'Thanks for the offer,' she told him. 'I'll bear it in mind.'

'Yes, I'm sure you will,' he said as anger sparked off inside him, 'then you'll forget about it. For goodness' sake, Amelie! You will have to get a local train at some ungodly hour to take you to the mainline station for a longish journey to the capital, followed by shoving and pushing on the tube or taking a taxi.

'It would be the same on your return journey, going through all that palaver again, unless your parents wanted to bring you back to Bluebell Cove in the family limo.'

She was smiling. 'You obviously know the stresses of getting to London and back off by heart. Of my parents you know nothing at all, or you wouldn't have made that last comment. I am not allowed to interfere in their lives, so if your offer is still there when the time comes, I will accept it gratefully.'

He would take her to the ends of the earth if need be, as long as they could be together. As for her parents, time would tell what he thought of them when he met them.

His mother now lived abroad with his sister. He loved them both dearly and they felt the same about him. There was nothing he wanted more than to show Amelie what proper family life was like, but their relationship was a fiasco at the present time.

It was a mellow Sunday in August when those involved in the christening of Freya Katherine Balfour arrived at the village church.

The name of Katherine had been chosen in respect of Phoebe's much-loved sister Katie, who had always been there for her in difficult times and shared her moments of rejoicing. Along with Jenna, she was to be the other of the baby's god-mothers, with Leo taking on the responsibilities of her godfather.

As the christening party walked to the front of the church, watched by the silent congregation, Phoebe's little boy, Marcus, was holding tightly onto Harry's hand and he was gazing down at him lovingly, while beside them Phoebe was car-rying the baby that she would soon be passing to the godparents in turn during the ceremony.

For Amelie, sitting as close as she could to the

font, there was a surprised smile from Leo that warmed her heart as he walked slowly past.

When he'd seen her and their glances had held, he'd thought tenderly how could he have ever thought she wouldn't be there? She was a part of this community now, with or without him, though he hoped that he was a part of the reason she had come to feel so at home there. When they arrived at the manor house afterwards, where there was a buffet laid on, he would take her to one side and…

They were taking up their positions in front of the font and the vicar was ready to start the service. His special time with Amelie would come later, he thought as he prepared to repeat the age-old words that would bind him to this child for ever.

Glades Manor was filled with well-wishers who had gone to share in the christening meal and the community spirit that was always there, be the gathering large or small.

The christening party had left before the rest of the congregation so as to be there to greet them when they arrived, and now Leo was searching for Amelie amongst the throng and telling himself with every passing second that she wasn't there.

Unbelievably, there was no sign of her and he thought grimly she must have seen her presence at the christening to be as much as she was prepared to be involved in on his behalf. So nothing had changed after all.

He was choking on the bitter taste of disappointment. Had Harry and Phoebe noticed her absence? he wondered. Probably not surrounded as they were by friends and well-wishers, and the rest of the surgery staff were enjoying themselves too much to notice that the young French doctor was giving the party a miss.

The urge to go and find out why she wasn't there was overwhelming but Phoebe had just put the baby in his arms and was about to take his photograph, and when that was done Harry and little Marcus were at his elbow, wanting to show him a new garden room that had just been added to the house.

So it was almost the middle of the afternoon before he could get away without offending anyone, and he drove to the village with the determination to find out if it was because of him she'd skipped the party.

He had part of the answer as soon as the house that Ethan had loaned her came into view. The car in the drive wasn't a limousine but it had the same luxurious kind of history and he didn't need to think twice about who it belonged to. It would seem that Amelie's wealthy parents had arrived.

They had to be the reason for Amelie's absence at the gathering at Glades Manor. He was ashamed that he had been so quick to judge. While turning the car round to go back to where he'd come from, she came to the door and waved for him to stop, then she was coming down the path towards him.

'I had a call on my mobile as I was coming out of church,' she explained, 'to say that my parents had arrived and were here outside the house. I couldn't get to you to explain and hurried back here to greet them.'

'Where are they now?' he asked in a low voice,

'Inside. I'm about to make a meal but it will be a scrappy affair as I wasn't expecting them.'

'Are you going to introduce me?' he wanted to know, with the thought that it was an ideal moment to get to know the strange Benoirs. Strange because they seemed to have had little time for their daughter, had put their jobs first, which was unthinkable to anyone who loved children.

She was observing him doubtfully. 'Do you want me to?'

'Does the sun rise and set? Of course I do. I'm interested in anything connected with you, and with regard to you making a meal at such short notice, why don't we take them to the christening party instead, to save you the trouble of cooking and to introduce your family to Harry and Phoebe and your other friends?'

'Do you think we should?' she queried doubtfully.

'Yes, I do. There's loads of food and it will give your parents a chance to see something of English country life with all its attractions.'

'All right, I'll suggest it to them, but first, if that is what you want, I'll take you to be introduced.'

He was laughing. 'So you're going to chance it. Take the risk?'

'It won't be a risk. They'll be dumbfounded to discover that I know someone like you.'

'So lead on and we'll take it from there,' he said with returning seriousness, while straightening his cuffs and wondering how the suit and tie would go down with her parents. Any other day than today he would have been in shorts and a cotton top, but the christening had called for more than that and so here he was dressed to kill, being introduced to two people that so far he had no cause to like.

He sensed that Amelie was on edge and as they entered the house he took her hand in his and gave it a squeeze that was meant to say, 'Don't worry. I'm going to marry you in any case,' but only ended up being what it was—a squeeze.

CHAPTER NINE

LISETTE and Charles Benoir were more or less what he'd expected them to be. Early fifties, smartly dressed, and very much in control of the situation, which was more than could be said of their daughter. Amelie's cheeks were flushed because where to some families there would be nothing strange in them turning up unexpectedly, clearly it was not the case with hers.

They were cordial enough when she introduced him to them and only by the flicker of an eyelid did either of them show surprise at the vision he presented.

It seemed that as Amelie hadn't been able to say exactly when she would be able to visit them in London, they had driven to Devon to seek her out and do some sightseeing at the same time.

She was clearly amazed that they'd made the effort and even more so when they'd graciously agreed to his suggestion that the four of them should join those still partying at Glades Manor—as long as their friends would have no objection, Charles Benoir stipulated.

'You have obviously shown some sense for once in coming to this place,' he said, addressing his daughter stiffly, with as good a command of the English language as hers.

Leo saw her mother flinch, watched the colour drain from Amelie's face, and in that moment all the loving protective tenderness he felt for her overwhelmed him. He'd felt the same way about Delphine. It had been there alongside the sexual chemistry, and now the kind fates were giving him a second chance to experience the wonder of that kind of love.

Maybe when Amelie understood the source of his caution she would forgive his behaviour. He hoped so. And as for the grumpy old guy who had just embarrassed her, he would take her away from that kind of thing if she would let him.

'What is *your* function in the community?' was Charles's next question.

'I am a partner in the village medical practice where your daughter is on loan to us at the moment,' he replied, and added, with a special smile in her direction, 'We will not be wanting her to leave us when the six months are up as Amelie is a very able member of the medical profession.'

'Ah! I see,' was the comment that greeted that information, and Leo wondered exactly what it was that Charles saw. But he was more interested in what Amelie had to say, and for the present she was saying nothing. The shock of finding her parents in Bluebell Cove and her father's sour manner were rendering her speechless.

It was always she who'd had to travel to them, so what had changed? She could tell they approved of Leo, his looks, his easy manner and the clothes he'd worn for the christening.

They must be wondering what part he played in her life, if any, and she thought wryly that she didn't know the answer to that herself. The only thing she was sure of was that she loved him and didn't know how to handle it.

The newcomers were made most welcome by Phoebe and Harry and when Amelie heard them ask her parents how long they were intending to stay, she was relieved to hear that it would be for just a couple of days before they headed off to Cornwall.

It was good to see them after a long absence, but she didn't want them butting into this pre-cious thing she had with Leo. One-sided it might be, but it was still very important.

When Leo was about to leave them in the early evening she went out to the car with him and he said in a low voice, 'What do you think has brought this on, coming all the way from London to see you?'

'I don't know,' was the answer, 'but there will

be a reason and it won't be because they were desperate to see me.'

'Don't say that,' he chided. 'None of us can choose our parents. Their manner may come from the kind of job they do. I felt sorry for your mother. She would seem not to have the same steel in her heart as your father. I take it that he rules the roost.'

'Yes, he does.' With pleading in her glance she went on, 'I wish you didn't have to go.'

'I can't intrude any longer into your reunion with them in spite of how flat it might be. Did you ask Harry if you could have the next two days off while they are here? I don't mind and I'm sure he won't.'

'No,' she said firmly. 'My parents have always put their job first, so I intend to do the same. I will be with them in the evenings, and during the day they intend to explore the coast and countryside.'

He was frowning. 'You can be quite inflexible when you want to be, Amelie.'

'Is that a reminder of when we were both fresh from the shower on the night we pulled Freddie from the sea?'

'It might be.'

'You don't understand, do you?' she said wearily. 'For as long as I can remember, I've felt unwanted, first by my parents and later by Antoine. Then I met you and everything was wonderful, until that night in the woods when I wanted us to make love and you rejected me. So is it surprising that I am not going to want to make that mistake again? If that seems inflexible, fine!'

She'd glanced over her shoulder a couple of times to make sure that Lisette and Charles hadn't been within earshot while she'd been opening her heart to him, but before he could reply to what she'd just said, she told him hurriedly, 'My parents must be thinking this is a long goodbye. I must go.'

'Yes, of course,' he agreed, reluctant to leave her after she'd explained her feelings so achingly and with such honesty. He said, 'It's been another day of mixed emotions, and it isn't over yet. So I'll leave you to catch up with what has been happening in your parents' lives, Amelie.' He smiled quizzically. 'Something tells me that you won't be in a hurry to tell them what has been happening in yours.' And with one last lingering look at the face that was still flushed and apprehensive, he pointed his car towards the apartments.

She wanted to run after him, throw herself into his arms, and, whether he wanted to hear it or not, tell him how he had changed her life, that she could endure anything her father had to say as long as he, Leo, was by her side, but that wasn't going to happen because they were waiting for her, seated in the back garden, watching a glorious sunset.

When she brought out a tray of drinks and joined them she had the strangest feeling of disquiet. Her father cleared his throat and said, 'We have sought you out because there is something that you have to be told.'

She thought, Here it comes, the reason they are here.

'Your mother and I are getting divorced,' he said without preamble, and she felt her jaw go slack.

'Why?' she gasped, and he actually managed a smile.

'Maybe we have seen too much of each other, working together as we have for so long,' he said, with a glance at her mother. 'We have both met other people and when the divorce comes through will be spending the rest of our lives with them.'

'You will be welcome to visit, of course,' her mother said hurriedly.

Amelie thought, Leo, where are you? Come and tell me I'm dreaming this. I'm on the outside of things again, the afterthought again.

Yet did she want him to come and see her like this, taken aback, distressed to be told that her parents' marriage was over? She'd seen little enough of them before, so what would it be like now?

She'd asked if they required separate bedrooms and when they'd said no, they would be fine, she couldn't believe it was happening, her parents about to divorce sleeping in the second-largest bedroom of the house where Ethan had told her she must feel free to have someone stay with her if she needed company. That her first house guests would be them had been the last thing she could have imagined.

When they'd gone up to bed she decided she had to get out of the house for a while to calm down. Letting herself out quietly, she began to walk to the place she loved best.

It wasn't yet midnight, there were still a few folks around, but when she reached the headland it was deserted and the Balfours' house was in darkness, which left her a solitary figure staring out to sea.

* * *

Leo had seen her come out of the house. He hadn't been able to settle after returning to the apartment and had stood gazing out of the window for a long time, wishing he hadn't left her so soon on this strange day of highs and lows.

When he saw that she was on the move he set off to follow her. There was no way he was going to let her go out into the night alone, especially in the direction of the headland and the beach, which were her favourite places, as they were his, but not at this time of night.

The purchase of Four Winds House was going through. In the last week he'd had it surveyed and paid a holding deposit, and though Keith wasn't going to get his wish before he went on his cruise, the sale would be well along the way by the time he came back.

When she heard a step behind her Amelie turned quickly. There had been no one around when she'd arrived and when she saw Leo standing there she couldn't believe it.

'What are you doing out here?' he asked gently. 'Is something wrong, Amelie?'

'Yes,' she sobbed. 'Didn't I tell you there would be a reason for my parents' visit? They're getting divorced and it's all so cold-blooded. Both of them are going to marry someone else. Knowing what they're like, I'm surprised they even bothered to tell me.'

'Whew!' he exclaimed. 'Was it on the cards?'

'Not that I knew of,' she told him between sobs, and when he tried to take her in his arms to comfort her she moved away and said chokingly, 'How do we know it would work out for us if you ever wanted me enough to marry me? I don't want to be hurt again.'

'You wouldn't be,' he assured her gently, with his new resolve firmly in place, but it was not the time or place to tell her about Delphine.

He held out his arms again but she wouldn't let him hold her close and, still sobbing, she said, 'How can I be sure? Half the time you don't want me near you, and the rest of the time you are everything I've ever dreamt of, so how do I cope with that sort of situation? Please, go away, Leo. I want to be alone.'

'All right,' he agreed grimly, 'but I'm not moving until you start making tracks for home. I shall be following you at a distance until I've seen you safely inside.'

'Please yourself,' she said wearily. 'Do whatever you think best, but leave me alone.'

He did as she'd asked once he'd seen her back where she belonged.

Back in the apartment, he was remembering that night at the airport when he'd gone to meet her and how he'd been disappointed and amazed that the odd-looking creature drifting sleepily towards him in the arrivals lounge was the young French doctor they were taking on at the surgery for six months.

They'd come a long way since then, but not as far as he wanted them to. Patience was still the name of the game, and after what Amelie had said about them back there on the headland, he might need plenty of it. In the meantime, he was going to do what she'd asked him to do, leave her alone for a while, and then when he felt she was ready he would tell her about Delphine, how at last he was ready to let her memory be a sweet and distant thing instead of a constant reminder of pain and grief.

After a sleepless night Amelie was up and about before her parents came down for the breakfast she'd prepared, and leaving them to clear away afterwards she was at the surgery in good time for Monday morning's overflow from the weekend.

When she and Leo met up again he was coming out of the staff kitchen with a mug of tea in his hand, and when she would have stopped to apologise for the way she'd told him to go the night before he didn't give her the chance. As the words trembled on her lips he wished her a brief good morning and disappeared into his consulting room, shutting the door behind him.

So much for that, he thought as he drank the tea. But how long was he going to be able to keep it up?

When a young guy who looked like a student presented himself in front of him in the late morning he looked far from well and was anxious to explain why he was there.

'I've been to a few late-night parties with my college friends over the last week,' he said, 'and I think I might have picked up some sort of virus. My throat is raw, I keep feeling faint, and I've got a rash.'

'Any aversion to bright lights?' was Leo's first question. The young man shook his head. 'Show me the rash, then.' And in keeping with the patient having no problem with a bright light, he concluded that it was not the dreaded red rash of meningitis.

'Does it itch?' was the next thing he wanted to know.

'Yes, a lot,' was the answer to that, and as

Leo examined it more closely he saw that there were red raised areas on the skin and where the patient had scratched them they'd turned to blisters.

'What have you been taking at these parties?' he questioned.

'If you mean drugs…nothing,' was the reply. 'My parents would go ballistic if I ever did that.'

'I was not referring to anything in particular,' he told him. 'Just trying to get a picture of what has caused this. Have you been on, or near a farm at all?'

'Er, yes. The parents of one of my mates have a farm. I was at a party there last week.'

'Did you handle any live stock on the farm?'

'I was around some cows that didn't look too lively.'

'Did you touch any of them?'

'I might have done, but why are you asking me all this?'

'It is possible that you might have contracted anthrax from the cattle. I'm going to take some blood samples and send them to the laboratory for a fast result.

'In the meantime, I'll give you something for your throat, which is very inflamed. Then go home, tell your parents what I've said, and that you have to rest until the results come through.

'There are two kinds of anthrax infection— cutaneous anthrax that affects the skin and is reasonably easy to cure, and pulmonary anthrax that affects the lungs and is much more serious. In your case, I would think from my experience of the illness that it is the less serious of the two.

'We will soon know if I'm right, and if I am the authorities will need the name of the farmer and the address of the farm as it will have to be inspected to see if the infection came from the animals themselves or from the land on which they were grazing, where it could have lain dormant for many years.

'I'll be in touch as soon as I have any news from the path lab. If it is what I suspect, we'll take it from there.'

By that time the youth was looking decidedly nervous, having got the picture of how rare anthrax infection was in humans and how serious it could be, and he went to do what he'd been told to do…rest, which was the only good thing about it. It gave him a very good reason for lying on top of his bed for hours on end, watching television.

For Amelie it was a morning of the usual things—a young pregnant woman with unpleasant morning sickness, a patient recently diagnosed with diabetes and suffering from the side-effects of the medication he'd been prescribed, which called for a change of plan, and an elderly woman who'd forgotten to take her blood-pressure medication with her on holiday and was desperate for reassurance that it wasn't out of control.

All of which she had given her full attention, but when one of the receptionists came round with elevenses and she had a few moments to herself, the flaws in her family life came flooding back and with them the memory of how she'd let Leo see how unsure she was of the future. She needed security like she needed to breathe.

She was deeply in love with him but wasn't sure of his reactions sometimes. And her parents, enjoying the delights of Devon, with Cornwall to come, would appear to have not given a second's thought to how she would react to their news.

Why she felt so upset about that she didn't know as she rarely saw them in any case, but the truth of the matter was that they'd spoilt it, taken away the wonderful feeling of security that had been hers ever since she'd come to Bluebell Cove and met Leo.

The vicar's wife had been in earlier, selling tickets for a hoe down on the coming Saturday night, and on impulse Amelie had bought one, without knowing what she was going to do with it as she wasn't in the mood for socialising.

Yet she could feel her batteries beginning to recharge after the upset of the night before. She was coming out of the slough of despondency. Her parents' insensitivity was not going to spoil her life any more, she told herself.

They were due back in the village from their stay in Cornwall early on Saturday evening and after a brief stop were driving back to London. So once they'd gone she was going to go to the hoe down.

It would be on her own as Leo had already demonstrated that he'd taken her demand to leave her alone seriously. So it would not be a night of nights or anything of that kind, but it would be better than staying in and moping.

In the days leading up to Saturday the young student with the rash had it diagnosed as the anthrax bacterium of the cutaneous type, which was treatable with penicillin. So he was still at home, resting and taking the medication, with Leo keeping a firm watch on his progress.

The hay-fever sufferers were paying the penalty of heavy pollen counts and the added problem of harvest reaping, which meant that theirs was a continuous presence in the waiting room. But for the rest of the population of Bluebell Cove there was a general air of well-being.

As the weekend drew near and still in a more positive frame of mind, Amelie was debating whether to buy tight jeans and a check shirt to wear for the hoe down. Having seen something along those lines in the window of the boutique, she decided to brave the cold stare of Leo's friend Georgina and go to try them on in her lunch hour.

The owner wasn't there, she was relieved to see. A young, brown-haired girl was serving and as she moved along the rails of fashionable clothes her enthusiasm was waning because it would normally have been Leo that she was out to please. But in the present state of affairs she didn't even know if he would be there.

Yet she already had the high leather boots to go with the clothes, and the jeans and shirt fitted perfectly when she tried them on, so those things and the fact that she felt she needed cheering up all combined to persuade her to buy, and moments later she left the shop with a spring in her step.

On Saturday night she was ready in good time. The clothes she'd bought looked good on her. She hadn't a hair out of place beneath a cowboy hat that she'd found in one of the cupboards in the house, and she thought wistfully that all she lacked was Leo. Without him, nothing was the same.

But he was still giving her some space, keeping as far away from her as possible out of working hours and during them acknowledging her presence only briefly.

She was waiting for her parents to arrive. She wasn't planning on going to the hoe down until they'd been and gone.

A flask of coffee and sandwiches for the journey were waiting for them. She knew her father wouldn't want to linger after he'd been for petrol to get them home and typical of the man their car pulled up outside the house at exactly the time he'd said it would, and as soon as he'd dropped her mother off he went to the garage.

The moment he had gone Lisette asked urgently, 'Do you love Leo Fenchurch, Amelie?'

'Yes,' she told her, surprised at the question. 'I love him more than life itself.'

Her mother nodded, as if that was what she wanted to hear, and went on to say, 'Then if he asks you to marry him, tell him yes. Turn your dreams into reality. That kind of love comes only once in a lifetime. Don't let it pass you by.'

Amelie was listening to what she was saying in complete bewilderment.

'Why are you telling me all this?' she asked.

'Because I know what that kind of love feels like,' Lisette replied, 'but mine was lost to me and I ended up marrying Charles.'

'And is that the reason why you're divorcing?'

'Yes, that's the reason. Charles doesn't think people should have feelings. Given the chance, he would exchange me for a robot without batting an eyelid.'

'So *my* feelings of rejection come from that tarnished point of view, do they?' Amelie said. 'Yet you've always gone along with it.'

'I had no choice because you are not his child,' was the incredible reply. 'He had always wanted me. Charles was head of my department, as he is now, and he said he would marry me and that I could keep you, as long as he came first in everything and you were always kept out of sight in the background. Does that explain what has happened over the years?'

Groping her way to the nearest chair, Amelie sank down on it. 'So who is my father?' she croaked.

'He was an Englishman called Robert Templeton. Robbie was killed in a skiing accident when I was four months pregnant. We were planning to be married before you were born. He was the only man I've ever loved, so you see why I say if Leo loves you as much as you love him and he asks you to marry him, don't hesitate.'

'I've got to be asked first,' she said flatly. 'And why are you telling me all this now after allowing me to feel so unwanted all my life?'

'Charles would never let me. He is a proud man and said he would throw both of us out if I told you, and it is he who is the wealthy one. I own nothing. But now I see you with this man and know it is the time to speak because I can tell he will love and protect you.'

They could hear the man she had known as her father all her life coming up the drive and Lisette said, 'He thinks I have found someone else but it isn't so. It's just an excuse to get away from him.

'There is just one thing before we leave,' she said pleadingly. 'If you marry your doctor, please let me come to the wedding.' Then, reverting back to her usual manner, she kissed her lightly on the cheek and went out to join her father, leaving Amelie to follow her to where their car was parked at the roadside as if nothing unusual had happened.

She went back inside on leaden feet and when the door closed behind her she knew she wanted Leo there to hold her, talk through with her what she'd just been told, but there'd been no sign of him at the apartment all day and the hoe down would have started by now. She could hear country and western music filtering through from the village hall.

As she stood irresolutely, fighting back tears, she saw him coming up the drive, and when she opened the door to him he looked at the clothes she was wearing and said, 'So you *are* intending going to the hoe down, Amelie. I was beginning to think you were giving it a miss.'

When she didn't answer he told her, 'I've stayed away from you for as long as I could but not any more. I saw your parents driving off as I was coming up the road. Was everything all right with them?'

Ironically, now he was there she found she couldn't speak; she was still in shock, so she just nodded and desperate to bring the moment back to normality picked up her handbag and her ticket for the hoe down and with a grimace of a smile pointed to the door.

CHAPTER TEN

As THEY walked the short distance to the village hall Leo glanced at her a few times and wondered what was wrong, but something told him not to press her to tell him.

It was significant that her parents had stopped off on their way back to London and had left Amelie in this state. Slow anger was kindling inside him at the thought of them bringing any more insecurity into her life.

On the other hand, the state she was in with her ashen face and the lack of response speechwise could be for some other reason than the Benoirs, yet he doubted it. He'd had plans for tonight, big ones, but with Amelie clearly emotional all he could do was register concern.

The hoe down was in full swing when they

got there, and a barn dance was in progress, so he took her out onto the village green and in the scented autumn night asked gently, 'Are you going to tell me what's wrong, Amelie? I've never seen you like this before. It's as if you're in shock.'

'Charles isn't my father,' she croaked, and he observed her incredulously.

'Who told you that?'

'My mother, the one person who is sure to know.'

'So that is what it's all about,' he said slowly. 'Why he's so crabby. Not all men have Harry Balfour's generosity of spirit. How do you feel about that?'

'I don't know,' she said raggedly. 'It was so unexpected I'm still in shock.'

'What made your mother tell you after all this time?'

'She didn't want me to make the mistakes she made.'

'And what were those?'

'Not marrying the man she loved and losing him in an accident, I suppose, then marrying a man she *didn't* love. It was all so sad, Leo.'

He reached out for her and held her close, and there were no requests to leave her alone this time. As he looked down on the shining crown of her dark head he said, 'The past creeps up on us when we least expect it, Amelie. I've made *my* peace with my past. Would you like to hear about it?'

'I suppose so,' she said listlessly, and he led her by the hand away from the noise to a bench outside the church and when they were settled he said, 'You are the only person I have ever spoken to about this.'

Her eyes widened, he had her full attention now. 'When I was twenty-five and in my last year at medical school I fell madly in love with one of my fellow students. Her name was Delphine and we were both of the same mind, that we wanted to spend the rest of our lives together, but it was not to be.

'Delphine had an undetected heart defect and in the middle of our wedding arrangements she was rushed into hospital with a cardiac arrest that proved fatal. The heartbreak and pain that followed her death were indescribable, feelings I've never forgotten. So much so that I've spent the last ten years on the social merry-go-round instead of putting down roots and having a family, because I didn't want to risk ever having to go through that again.

'But then you came along and changed my life for ever. Being with you, falling in love with you, didn't feel like a risk, it felt like it was heaven sent, yet still I was haunted by the past. But not any more, Amelie. Finally I'm free of the guilt and of the fear, free to tell you how much I love and adore you.'

There were tears in her eyes. 'Couldn't you have told me about Delphine before?' she asked gently. 'I would have understood you so much better. Poor Delphine. Poor you.'

'Yes,' he agreed. 'I won't ever forget her but it

will be without the nightmare that I've carried around with me all this time. I am ready to move on if you'll only say you love me.'

The bluebell eyes looking into his would have been enough answer but she asked tenderly, 'How many times would you like me to say it? Ten, twenty, a thousand times, or more?'

'More,' he murmured with his lips against her hair. And then he was kissing her, and kissing her, until she said breathlessly, 'I can't believe that only an hour ago I was feeling so miserable, yet now I have a father who would have loved me had he lived, and a better understanding with my mother, but you are my true joy-bringer, Leo, with your love and tenderness and the desire you arouse in me. The Angel Gabriel would find you a hard act to follow.'

He was smiling at the comparison and, taking her hand, he brought her to her feet and asked, 'Can you smell food, Amelie? They will be serving supper at the hoe down about now, and it is always a feast of delight, so shall we join them?

And then, afterwards, would you like to go for a drive?'

'Absolutely,' she replied dreamily. 'Whatever you say.'

For the first time in her life she was totally content and it was all due to the man beside her. He hadn't asked her to marry him yet, but she felt sure he would when he was ready.

The meal was, as Leo had said it would be, a feast, with cheeses galore and fresh vegetables from village gardens served as salads and soups, along with ham from the pig farms and fruit from the trees, and fresh loaves from the bakery, crispy and warm.

They sat with Harry and Phoebe and their two little ones, and while the two women chatted the head of the practice said to Leo, 'So have you been to fix it with the bellringers yet, and suggested to Ethan that he gets a season ticket for crossing the Channel? Since he went to live in France he's been over here more than he's been over there.'

'Is it so obvious?' he replied laughingly. 'We have to fix a date first, but it won't be long, I hope.'

It became clear that Leo hadn't meant a lazy cruise around the neighbourhood when he'd suggested they go for a drive as the road signs indicated that he was heading for the airport.

Minutes later they were parking there and as she stood gazing around her on the tarmac he said, 'This way, Amelie.' She followed him to the arrivals lounge. The walkway from the aircraft was deserted, as he had hoped it would be, and as she observed him questioningly he went down on one knee and said, 'This is the place where my life began again. Will you marry me, Amelie?'

She was laughing, joyful peals of delight. 'Yes, please,' she cried, and if she'd had any ideas that the request might have been impulsive rather than planned, he opened his clenched palm and revealed a solitaire diamond ring.

'I bought it weeks ago,' he told her. 'Yet the chance to ask you never seemed to materialise, but now all our problems are sorted, so how soon can I put a band of gold on your finger next to the diamond, Amelie?'

'Soon.' She glowed. 'I would like to be married while it's still harvest-time if possible. How long does it take to get a licence?'

'And a memorial plaque.'

'What for?'

'For *this* spot, to commemorate *this* event, if the airport authorities will allow it,' he teased. 'And now come here, my lovely French doctor, and let me show you how much I love you.' As he kissed his wife-to-be a cheer went up from the curious and the romantics who had been gathering to watch.

As they approached the village on their way home, Leo pulled up across the way from the headland and said, 'I have something to tell you,

Amelie. Would you like to get out of the car for a moment?'

Taking her hand, he took her to the same spot where they'd met unexpectedly on the night that her father had told her about the divorce. Turning her towards the solitary house that once again was in darkness as Keith was still on his cruise, he said, 'This will be my wedding present to you.'

Her eyes were round pools of amazement. 'You mean that we...'

'Yes, I mean that we are going to live here. I bought this house for us. I know how much you love the water and this house has the best sea views of anywhere in Bluebell Cove. The sale is going through and as I'm a first-time buyer it shouldn't take long. Would you like to wait until it is ours before we marry, or just set a date now and hope it might have gone through when the day arrives?'

'I'd rather wait,' she said joyfully, 'so that

we can start our life together in this wonderful house.'

'Me too,' he said, holding her close. 'And now I'm going to take you home to bed in your posh lodgings, then it will be bed for me too in the apartment, and soon I won't ever have to do that again.'

EPILOGUE

SEPTEMBER was almost gone, October was waiting at the gate, and the house was finally theirs. The sale had gone through smoothly and they'd been sure enough of its completion to fix a date and arrange their wedding.

The church was full and if there were some present who wondered how the young French doctor had managed to capture Leo Fenchurch, they needed only to observe his expression as Amelie appeared on the arm of Charles Benoir, dressed in a white wedding gown that set off her dark tresses and clung to her slender curves.

There were no bridesmaids, but Phoebe Balfour, with whom Amelie had become firm friends, was her matron of honour and Harry was Leo's best man.

His mother and sister were there from abroad, and on being introduced to her new mother-in-law who, though frail, had the same looks and personality as her son, Amelie had felt that here was a kindred spirit.

Her own mother was seated in one of the front pews, elegant and withdrawn on the outside but inside rejoicing that it was all coming right for her daughter.

She and Charles had brought a very special wedding present with them for Amelie and her new husband. It was the news that the divorce was off. They'd both only been fantasising about having someone else and had decided to stay together because they'd been partners too long to change their ways, and if they'd never thought her to be particularly striking before, today their daughter, Amelie, looked radiant and would continue to be so because she and Leo had reached out and taken hold of the kind of love that lasted for ever.

The evening reception, the final part of the

wedding festivities, was over. Their special day was coming to an end, but not yet. They'd arrived at the house and after he'd unlocked the door Leo bent and, picking Amelie up in his arms, carried her over the threshold and up into a large bedroom with a breathtaking view of the sea.

Laying her gently on the bed, he looked down on her and said softly, 'It's been a long journey for us both, Amelie. But at last we are together, and if I have my way we'll stay here in Bluebell Cove for ever.'

Amelie smiled up at her handsome new husband. 'This place has healed us both. I could never consider being anywhere else. I came here because I was running away, but instead I have finally come home, and that is all because of you, Leo. I do love you so much.'

'And I love you, my beautiful French wife.' And with his eyes darkening with tenderness and desire, 'Now I'm going to show you just how much, Amelie, because we're in the right place and it's the right time.'

And after that it felt as if there was only the sea, the sand and the two of them in the whole wide world.

* * * * *

Mills & Boon® Large Print Medical

October

TAMING DR TEMPEST	Meredith Webber
THE DOCTOR AND THE DEBUTANTE	Anne Fraser
THE HONOURABLE MAVERICK	Alison Roberts
THE UNSUNG HERO	Alison Roberts
ST PIRAN'S: THE FIREMAN AND NURSE LOVEDAY	Kate Hardy
FROM BROODING BOSS TO ADORING DAD	Dianne Drake

November

HER LITTLE SECRET	Carol Marinelli
THE DOCTOR'S DAMSEL IN DISTRESS	Janice Lynn
THE TAMING OF DR ALEX DRAYCOTT	Joanna Neil
THE MAN BEHIND THE BADGE	Sharon Archer
ST PIRAN'S: TINY MIRACLE TWINS	Maggie Kingsley
MAVERICK IN THE ER	Jessica Matthews

December

FLIRTING WITH THE SOCIETY DOCTOR	Janice Lynn
WHEN ONE NIGHT ISN'T ENOUGH	Wendy S. Marcus
MELTING THE ARGENTINE DOCTOR'S HEART	Meredith Webber
SMALL TOWN MARRIAGE MIRACLE	Jennifer Taylor
ST PIRAN'S: PRINCE ON THE CHILDREN'S WARD	Sarah Morgan
HARRY ST CLAIR: ROGUE OR DOCTOR?	Fiona McArthur

Mills & Boon® Large Print Medical

January

THE PLAYBOY OF HARLEY STREET	Anne Fraser
DOCTOR ON THE RED CARPET	Anne Fraser
JUST ONE LAST NIGHT…	Amy Andrews
SUDDENLY SINGLE SOPHIE	Leonie Knight
THE DOCTOR & THE RUNAWAY HEIRESS	Marion Lennox
THE SURGEON SHE NEVER FORGOT	Melanie Milburne

February

CAREER GIRL IN THE COUNTRY	Fiona Lowe
THE DOCTOR'S REASON TO STAY	Dianne Drake
WEDDING ON THE BABY WARD	Lucy Clark
SPECIAL CARE BABY MIRACLE	Lucy Clark
THE TORTURED REBEL	Alison Roberts
DATING DR DELICIOUS	Laura Iding

March

CORT MASON – DR DELECTABLE	Carol Marinelli
SURVIVAL GUIDE TO DATING YOUR BOSS	Fiona McArthur
RETURN OF THE MAVERICK	Sue MacKay
IT STARTED WITH A PREGNANCY	Scarlet Wilson
ITALIAN DOCTOR, NO STRINGS ATTACHED	Kate Hardy
MIRACLE TIMES TWO	Josie Metcalfe

Discover Pure Reading Pleasure with

Visit the Mills & Boon website for all the latest in romance

Buy all the latest releases, backlist and eBooks

Find out more about our authors and their books

Join our community and chat to authors and other readers

Free online reads from your favourite authors

Win with our fantastic online competitions

Sign up for our free monthly eNewsletter

Tell us what you think by signing up to our reader panel

Rate and review books with our star system

www.millsandboon.co.uk

 Follow us at twitter.com/millsandboonuk

 Become a fan at facebook.com/romancehq